Chronicles of the Realm Wars

DARKEST HOUR

Chris Schuler

PublishAmerica
Baltimore

First printing

ISBN: 1-4241-3622-9
PUBLISHED BY PUBLISHAMERICA, LLLP
www.publishamerica.com
Baltimore

Printed in the United States of America

Dedication

To my grandparents, who were always there for me, come hell or high water. It was, after all, my grandma that convinced me to follow my dreams of writing with a gift of a dictionary and a few notebooks. I still have them.

Acknowledgments

I would like to thank my family: my parents, who somehow managed to scrape up the money to send five kids to private schools; my little brothers, Tony, Nick, and Bobby, whom I look to for inspiration; and my sister Melissa, who manages to keep her sanity in a home ruled by boys.

I would also like to make a shout out to the other three members of the fantastic four: Jacob, Tony, and Trevor. We did everything together through high school, and they became the best friends a guy could have.

History of the Realm Wars

In the beginning there were only the four gods in the Realm of the Living, Jipniv, Motka, brother Kouja, and sister Sinji. All four lived among the earth, creating and twisting the land to their will. Coming together it was decided amongst the gods that worshipers were needed to build the massive temples and castles that were only fitting for the gods. Thus, the races were made. The gods turned to their new creations and said: "Go now and build yourselves a mighty civilization, so that you may repopulate and fill the earth. When your numbers are greater your species shall serve us; working to worship our divinity."

Thus it was done. Grand cities of silver sprouted from the land, farmers marched out into the untamed fields and tilled the land, settling the wilds with hoe and spade. When the earth had been populated the four gods each took a fourth of the inhabitants for themselves; then, with their newly created worshipers, the gods ordered them to build.

Jipniv, a lover of ancient forests and all things green, ordered his people to create a city of trees and slow-running brooks. Clothed in cloth of green silk the worshipers of Jipniv worked the wilderness, bending it to their will.

Motka, a god of solid stature and a love for great strength, ordered his people to burrow deep into the mountains, to craft imposing caverns, and to mine the many minerals of the earth; jewels, silver, bronze, and gold, which he loved above all. His temples became impregnable fortresses amidst the snow-capped mountains.

Kouja, a god of practicality, took his followers to the fields of the south, telling them to cultivate the land, and to build cities that stretched across the horizon. His worshipers grew in number and after many years his race of followers dwarfed all the others combined; although they had fallen behind in the arts and in technology.

Sinji was the youngest and vainest of the gods. A lover for beauty and magic, she brought her people to the islands deep in the south to live in a tropical paradise. Her temple was built beneath the waves, crafted by those she had gifted with fins and gills.

Thousands of years of prosperity and growth passed, each god growing in power with every advancement of their worshipers. Sitting beneath the waves in her temple of coral Sinji grew jealous of the other gods. Motka grew rich as his stockpiles of gold and gems grew at his feet, and Jipniv held a knowledge that far surpassed hers. Years passed and yet she was never content. As time passed she began to craft an evil plan.

Visiting her brother in his great city Sinji offered an alliance. Kouja did not agree with the plan at first, but Sinji was skilled with words and soon her sibling fell to her promises of great power. In secret they built an army, the first the world had ever seen. Armed with blunt weapons and simple leather armor the armies of the two siblings invaded the kingdoms of their enemies.

The attack surprised and soon overwhelmed the other two gods. Jipniv's green sanctuaries where burned to the ground, and the mighty halls that had sat in the mountains where ground to dust, the hordes of precise metals stolen or lost to the depths. However, Jipniv and Motka were clever gods, and halted the advance of the religion-driven warriors.

Motka's worshipers excelled in working with rock and metal, the pure elements of the earth. They crafted deadlier weapons—swords and axes—and pounded metal thin so that it could be worn over one's shoulders. His mighty fortresses of rock proved difficult to take and withstood even the most savage of assaults.

The followers of Jipniv where quick and agile, hiding in the forests to strike at their invaders with bows and spears. Sorcerers controlled the elements of nature, sending wild animals clawing at the enemy, and even uprooting giant trees and sending them into battle on feet made of roots.

The battle raged, millions perished and the great cities and structures were erased from the face of the earth. Many technologies were lost forever; the war took more from the races than just their lives. At last, on a final climatic battle on the very edge of the Vulscar Canyon, Sinji and her brother where defeated. As punishment for their crimes, the two gods were cast below the surface of the earth along with all of their followers.

Because of injuries received in battle Jipniv and Motka decided in all their holiness to leave the Realm of the Living to create a new home. This they called the Realm of the Second Life. If their followers lived a holy life, and worshiped unconditionally, their souls would come to this perfect place upon their death. But, if these conditions were not met, their damned souls would fall to the Realm of the Dead to be manipulated by the evil gods.

Excerpt from El Inu's Esnt'a
First Book of the Sun Gods

Prologue
Four Years Before the Story

Lightning flashed as a lone figure dressed in black guided his horse through the woods. His face remained hidden beneath his hood, heavy metal gauntlets clutched at the reins, barely holding on from the fatigue that coursed through his veins. Dark blotches covered the figure's clothes; more of the blackness ran down the center of a large broadsword that remained clasped to the horse's side. The warhorse could barely move ahead; a multitude of cuts and gashes oozed from its flank.

Wind howled like a caged animal, marking the coming of a storm. Trees leaned heavily to the side, fighting with all of their will to stay upright. For some even that was too much. Screeching in agony the age-old organisms crashed to the ground. Raindrops began to splatter against the earth. Only a few at first, but increasing in number until it turned into a downpour. The figure did not seem to notice and continued moving at his slow pace.

Breaking from the tree line the man found himself entering the field on which a battle had raged only a few short hours ago. Bodies littered the ground, broken spears jutted from the soft soil, shattered shields cracked and rattled beneath the steed's hooves. Without giving the corpses a second glance the figure continued forwards. The dead seamed to stretch on forever. Thousands lay dead. Not a soul moved. Not one single wounded soldier lifted an arm and begged for help. The only sound came from the storm.

The rain fell harder, the wind blew with a newfound savagery, and the lightning turned the night into day.

Suddenly, bringing his steed to a stop, the figure looked up at the looming structure that pierced the pouring rain. A stone pyramid made of overlapping squares of decreasing size stretched into the sky. Bodies covered the steps as the battle had pushed through. A large flag of shredded cloth flapped in the wind, a beacon calling for the figure's attention. Dismounting he began the long climb to the top.

Halfway up the side of the pyramid the man clothed in black stopped to look down on the field once more, as if considering regret, but then he turned his back to the destruction and continued forward, a renewed vigor in his step.

At the uppermost section of the pyramid water poured from the corners, water puddled in the center where a five-pointed star had been carved into the stone years, nay, millennia ago. Five runes, each at one point of the star, were also carved, but the language of these runes had been lost for centuries. A stone gargoyle sat on each corner, mouth open, snarling and revealing rows of pointed teeth.

Halting on the edge of the pyramid's apex the figure waited, standing perfectly still in the rain as his cloak billowed behind him as if attempting to escape from the evil that surrounded this place.

Flames burst in the mouths of the gargoyles, their stone eyes began to burn an evil red. The star and the runes on the top of the pyramid also burst into flames, burning brightly despite the driving rain. The wind grew in strength until it became a roar. Then, as suddenly as it had begun, the flames died away and the wind escaped with it. No sound remained but the steady pitter-patter of the rain.

Then with a loud crack an object slammed into the top of the pyramid, throwing a cloud of water droplets in all directions. Unprepared for the blast the figure fell over backwards, rolling down several of the steps before forcing himself to stop. Quickly scrambling back to the top of the pyramid he looked calmly at what rose up from the pyramid's center.

The creature had no shape, as if it had dimmed so that its skin could not be seen. A pattern appeared through the rain as the water fell on the creature's shoulders. A long snout poked out, shedding water in two huge rivers. A loud hiss issued forth; a snake-like whine. Taking a step the invisible daemon carefully eyed the mortal that stood before it.

"For what purpose do you call me?" it demanded.

"I have done as the goddess has requested. I seek what is mine."

"And what, pray tell, is it that you claim to be yours?"

"Power."

The daemon laughed, a deep booming that rivaled even the thunder that crashed in the violent night sky. "Is that all you mortals think about? All you crave is power yet you never know how to harness it."

"I was told by the goddess—" The man began to protest before being cut off.

"The goddess knows what she has promised!" the creature screamed, throwing the man back a few steps. Then, the daemon seemed to calm itself. "You will have what you seek. But, there is still more for you to do."

"More?"

"Yes, the Southlands are ripe for the picking. Their demise will be your uprising. Defeat these scum, and release the goddess from her condemning prison, and you will become more powerful than you can even imagine."

"How am I to release the goddess?"

"Now is not the time to know. Crush the South and the truth shall be revealed."

"I will not fail." The man thumped his fist against his chest, saluting the daemon that stood before him.

"Even now the blood of the North's old king stains your blade, a symbol of your allegiance to the goddess of blood. You are now king of all the Northlands. Raise an army and smite the South. The state of war that has lasted between the two kingdoms for five hundred years is drawing to a close. The end…is near!" The daemon then pointed a menacing finger. "Do not fail," it ordered.

With a bright flash of lightning the daemon disappeared, leaving in its place a shining crown of gold. Even in the darkness it glowed with an unnatural brilliance.

Chapter 1
The Prisoner

The sun had barely risen to signify the beginning of the day, but for the wounded soldiers that lay in the wagons it seemed to have already lasted a month. Healers walked solemnly among them, offering what little care they could provide, weeping silently for the more seriously wounded who lay in silence, eyes beginning to glaze over. There was little that they could do until the convoy reached Thuringer. The drivers forced their horses to move at a snail's pace, but the road was filled with hidden rocks and pits which jerked and jarred the wagons violently; screams rose up from the wounded with each movement as broken bones shifted and old wounds reopened.

Steam puffed from the muzzles of the teams, sweat glistened on overheated bodies. Clouds of white smoke, swirling and dancing in the freezing air, flowed from their backs. With every step the four-legged beasts shook, begging for a rest. The drivers ignored the silent pleas of their teams for there would be no rest until Thuringer had been reached.

Sitting in one of the rocking wagons, wrapped in a blood-stained blanket, Seramin watched as still-dormant farmhouses passed in the dim light. The early farmers still had yet to come out and tend to the daily chores. He thought of his family; in another hour they would all be climbing from their beds, his son would feed the animals while his daughter would milk the cows, collect eggs from the chickens, and gather firewood. His wife would clean the house and would then prepare breakfast. Gods, he missed them!

Reaching in his pocket the wounded captain brought out a small golden coin and held it tightly in his hand. Closing his eyes he began to pray to the sky gods for the protection of his family. One of the other wounded soldiers in the wagon watched the silent ritual with curiosity.

"What's that you got there?"

"Huh?" Seramin's head jerked upright.

"That. There in yer hand. What is it?"

"Nothing." Seramin quickly stuffed the coin back into his pocket. The picture of a dragon with outstretched wings and fire spewing from its mouth was carved into the coin's surface. On the other side were several strange-looking runes. But the man did not see that.

"It looked pretty," the man remarked, trying to make conversation.

"Thanks."

"What happened to you?" he ventured to question after the moments passed. Asking others about their wounds had become a favorite way of passing the long hours among the wounded.

"Arrow in the shoulder." Seramin pointed with his good hand. "And then a spear in the back a few days later."

"Ay, that must have hurt. Myself, I got my arm lopped off during the battle on the Yatze River." Pulling the stump free from his blanket the man waved it in the air for all to see. "A big bloke got it with the axe, but I managed to finish him off in the end."

"I'm sorry," Seramin muttered. He didn't know what else he could say to the poor man.

"Bah!" The man waved the stump again before tucking it away. A big grin split his unshaven face; two rows of yellowed teeth leapt out from the dull brown beard. "There is many a man who is worse off than I. But, I would be feeling more sorry for yerself."

"Me?"

"Ay, your wounds aren't so bad as far as I can see, and soon you'll be back in the front lines again."

Seramin didn't want to think about that possibility, but the man was probably right. Once his wounds had healed the army would send him right back into the thick of battle. Back to the bloody meat grinder that had taken the lives of so many soldiers in the past two years. Seramin had outlived many of his comrades; even as their bodies piled around his feet, arrows jutting from squirming bodies, axes splitting skulls as if they were eggshells.

The soldiers in the wagons had been the lucky ones, those that had been found among the fields of dead before the hand of death had found them. Winter was very convenient in that it killed off the wounded in utter silence. A few hours in the bitter cold and one would be rock solid, a giant block of reddish ice.

The captain frowned. How many men had marched to war while leaving their loved ones behind such as he had? Too many. The evidence glared at the army as they marched through the towns and villages; women and children stared back with hollowed eyes, not a single husband or father in sight. War had become a parasite. It fed on the males, sucking them into its deep gullet while calling for more to fill its inexhaustible hunger.

Just then, over the final hill of the voyage, a magnificent city of silver came into view. The convoy had reached Thuringer at last.

Surrounded on all sides by a tall wall constructed of white stone and a shallow moat, the city was the pride and joy of the South. Not only the capital and home of the king, but a near-impregnable fortress. Inside the wall was a large section of the city: homes, shops, and barracks packed tightly together like sardines. Behind this a second wall and another moat lay in wait, followed by more buildings, and then the castle itself. The sun crawled up behind the city and the walls sparkled brilliantly. In the early morning light the shine of spears and halberds could be seen on the wall ledge as guards patrolled the perimeter, searching tirelessly for any sign of intruders.

Seramin twisted around so that he could get a better view of the city. This was his birthplace, the city where he had spent his childhood as the only kin of a poor iron worker. His mother had died while giving birth, abandoning him to a merciful, kind, and loving father. Seramin had learned the trade of a blacksmith, becoming quite skilled in the trade, but when the call for soldiers had come he had signed up with reckless abandon, against the wishes of his pacifist father. He needed a life of adventure, something he would never get as a blacksmith.

Moving swiftly through the ranks Seramin proved himself as a master swordsmen and an able leader. He was a sergeant even before his first battle. Two years of campaigns in the orcish lands had revealed the hardships of warfare. A veil had been pulled from the butchery that had been hidden from him at first. He came to hate violence, and to loathe the army.

Now his own family lived only a day's ride to the south. A twelve-year-old boy with sparkling blue eyes and his father's old thirst for adventure. A little girl of seven years, quiet, yet brilliant in her silence. Lastly, a beautiful wife, one who loved children more than all of the riches in the world, a woman that cuddled with them every night and whispered stories of Dwarves and Elves into their ears as the fell into sleep.

As the convoy edged closer small holes and cracks in the outer wall could be seen. They were the result of catapults an invading Northern army had used to siege Thuringer over five hundred years ago. According to legend, the siege had lasted two months and the first wall had been breached, the second had nearly been overwhelmed, but the invading army had been defeated and the city saved.

By the outer moat a tall marble tower stood with a copper plaque attached to its base. The inscription told of the terrible siege, and praised the brave defenders that had perished in order to protect their homeland. The might of the Southern empire lived on because of them. All had been saved by the men's unselfish sacrifice in the name of the sun gods.

As the sun rose higher into the sky peasants began to emerge from their homes and began the daily rituals that ruled their lives. The convoy distracted them for a moment, but they turned away for they had grown accustomed to the horrors that the war had brought upon them. At first, the wounded soldiers had been praised by large crowds and showering rose petals. Now only silence welcomed them. Two years of war had crushed the people's enthusiasm for the conflict.

Seramin watched the inky black waters of the moat as they passed over the creaking drawbridge. The water bubbled and croaked as it flowed swiftly, as black and swift as death. Chunks of ice, spinning feebly in the clutches of a greater power, cried for help. Some sank beneath the surface, a hazy cloud of white; some disappeared altogether.

Entering the second wall the convoy came to a rest and was met by a small crowd of healers who carefully lifted the wounded and began to transport them to the Healer's Guild. There the men would be given herbs and small doses of magic in order to heal their wounds. The most seriously injured were carried in makeshift stretchers, screaming as they where hauled away. Trails of steaming blood fell in the frozen snow.

Gritting his teeth Seramin slowly lowered himself to the ground. The spear wound in his lower back was shallow, but with every movement that he made the torn flesh began to burn like a red-hot poker. The one-armed men hopped down beside him, wounded arm once again hidden beneath the blanket. "Good luck to ye," he said offering his left arm in an awkward handshake.

Seramin just nodded.

"The name's Timmy, by the way, in case you ever want to get together and join me and the boys for a drink." Timmy still held out his hand.

"I'll think about it," Seramin gave an awkward smile, refusing the handshake, "but I really don't drink."

"You will, trust me. War is more than enough to make a man drink his guts out."

Timmy flashed another grin and then hobbled off in the direction of the guild.

Seramin had barely taken a step when he was met by a wall of red.

Clothed in blood-red capes a full dozen royal guards, metal armor shining in the dim light and long swords resting easily on their hips, stared down at the injured captain with uneasy coolness. Heavy medallions made of silver swung to and fro from their necks. Runes translating to "To the Glory of the Gods" bit deeply into the metal.

"Captain Seramin?" the tallest and most imposing guard asked as if already knowing the answer.

"Yes?" Seramin's hand instinctively reached for the handle of his sword, then he willed the nervous appendage away. The guards glanced at the movement, and then focused once again on the captain's face. They had seen enough soldiers from the front line to expect such a response.

"I am Litter Mongel of the royal guards. King Terin requests your presence immediately."

Seramin was taken back by the directness of the guard. Why would the king want to see him? He was tired, in pain, and didn't really want to see anyone at the moment. Not even the king. Especially in his current state.

"I respect the king's wishes, but as you can see I am injured from battle and need rest. Perhaps I could meet the king tomorrow."

"I'm sorry, Captain, but the king has made it crystal clear that he must meet you today." The guard gave a wordless signal and the other bodyguards formed a circle around Seramin. He looked at their faces, searching for a weakness, for a chance to plead his case. Only statue-like faces looked back at him.

Breathing a heavy sigh Seramin turned to the leader, holding back his annoyance. "I have just returned from the front and I am not ready to meet the king at this moment."

"I understand your position, Captain," the royal guard smiled cruelly when he looked down on Seramin's rank bars on his shoulder, "and to be frank I really don't care. I've seen enough front-line soldiers and wounded to lose all sense of empathy. Now, come along, or my men will be forced to use force."

"I'd like to see you say that when I have two good arms."

"I doubt any of us will live that long. Now…" Stepping aside the man gave a formal invitation for Seramin to proceed with a wave of his arm.

Seeing no other choice Seramin snatched his crutch from the wagon and hobbled along with the guards. His movements still remained painful and it took a great amount of care to keep up with the pace that the guards set. Several of them rolled their eyes and mumbled under their breath about how Seramin was keeping them out in the freezing weather longer than they preferred. Hearing their complaints Seramin slowed his movement even further, pretending to stumble and slip through the snow.

"Anyone mind telling me what this is about?" the captain asked, a bit too angrily.

"I'm sorry, but only the king can tell you that."

"But I don't understand…"

"You will in a moment, I assume."

The castle was a huge building surrounded by an equally massive garden. Tall bushes lined marble walkways and frozen ponds sat by empty plots that held all breeds of flowers in the spring. Royal guards stood everywhere, their red uniforms a brilliant contrast against the green bushes and white snow. Like gigantic holly berries. Since the onset of the war the king had grown fearful of assassins and the royal guards had been posted everywhere. Tiring of his slow progress the guards shoved Seramin none too gently through the entrance of the castle.

The first thing that he noticed was the absolute silence that dominated the long and spectacular halls. Reddish-colored stone pillars supported a tall ceiling; oversized oil paintings and lavish tapestries flowed down the walls and onto the floor. At regular intervals braziers sat in sandstone basins, lighting the way and providing warmth from the bitter cold outside.

"This way."

The captain followed. It seemed that he had no other choice in the matter.

Dark mahogany doors with ornamental markings, smooth stone walls, and expertly carved statues flashed by in a blur. They moved up several flights of stairs and then passed through double doors into a long hallway lit by windows that stretched from floor to ceiling. These windows overlooked the city, and Seramin had to resist the temptation to stop and stare at the sight.

At the end of the hallway a final door stood; this one larger than any of the others that Seramin had seen. Two more royal guards stood at attention at the entrance, but didn't flinch as Seramin and his escort bustled past. They had been briefed about this dirty, blood-stained veteran.

Seramin's heart leapt into his throat at what he saw through the doors. The captain now stood in the king's conference room. Circular in shape with fourteen large pillars spaced out in even intervals, the room dwarfed any others in the castle. Four massive stained-glass windows snuggled into the stone walls, sending beams of light to illuminate the center of the room where a lush and comfortable throne sat atop a raised platform of overlapping circular disks.

The floor surrounding the chair consisted of decorated copper grating that had been designed to depict ancient battles between long-forgotten enemies. His feet clanged noisily against the metal, cutting through the silence. Looking down Seramin saw only darkness. A tangible dread wafted up from the unknown. It was as if something terrible and brooding lay right beneath his feet. The captain turned to the leader of the royal guards. They had not entered the room, as if afraid to enter. Some glanced nervously over their shoulders. "Wait here, the king will be with you in a moment," the leader said. He punched his fist to his chest in salute.

Seramin could only return the salute; sloppily.

When the guards had left he looked down at his miserable state of dress. After serving in the field for so long his uniform had become tattered beyond recognition, and dripped with filth. His clothes smelled horrible; a combination of sweat, blood, gore, and human waste. He scraped at his clothes, trying to clean up his wardrobe, but then gave up realizing that the situation was hopeless.

Looking around the massive chamber Seramin noticed something that he had missed before. The pillars did not touch the surrounding wall, but rather stood ten feet from a circular walkway surrounding the chamber. This section of the floor was not grated, but rather solid stone. On the wall a large collection of paintings burned like expensive gemstones. Some appeared shiny and well cared for, others dirty and neglected. Limping over to the largest Seramin examined it closely.

Two massive armies were in the midst of battle, hundreds of thousands of warriors from each side climbed down the sides of a rocky valley, their intentions to destroy their adversaries. The army on the right dressed primarily in blue and green, while the one on the left wore red and black. In the far right of the painting stood two dominating figures. One was surrounded by a blue aurora and took the form of a large creature seeming to be made of stone; a green light surrounded the other that was in the form of a goat-like animal with large curved horns and pulsing white fur.

In the left of the painting stood the leaders of the red and black army. They had the images of an overly large snake and a man entirely encased in black armor. They pointed to the forces of good and urged their minions forward.

Gaping into the painting Seramin thought that he could see real fire burning in the eyes of the evil leaders. The painting crackled with evil and good in its battle for dominance. Magic flowed through the canvas.

"That's my favorite painting," a raspy voice said.

Spinning around Seramin came face to face with King Terin, the ruler of the Southern realm. Dressed in a long purple robe topped with a shining crown on his head the king appeared to be a hundred years old. Wrinkles covered a troubled brow and a thick mane of white hair flowed from beneath the crown. His eyes were grey and distant looking. A skeletal form dissolved into a purple sea.

"Your majesty!" Seramin cried as he attempted to kneel, but instantly became wracked with pain.

"There is no need," the king reassured, "your wounds are proof enough of your loyalty." Seramin staggered to his feet, but did not say anything, allowing the king to speak. "I am sure you are wondering why you are here, Captain?"

"That I am, your grace. Why is it that you demand my presence, a lowly soldier instead of a general?" He chose his words carefully, making sure not to mention his earlier resentment for his rapid summoning. Now being in the presence of the king Seramin's anger dissolved.

"A lowly soldier?" the king asked in surprise. "I too served in the army in my day, and my boy, I can assure you that a captain is in no way a meaningless position."

"What could I possibly tell you of the front that the entire kingdom does not know of already, much less yourself?"

"I seek no knowledge from you; I know everything that I kneed to know."

"You do?" Seramin was confused; why was he here then?

"Of course I do." Shuffling across the room the king ascended to his throne and threw himself down, giving out a loud sigh as his old bones cracked back into place. "You are Captain Puat Seramin. You led the infamous charge through the swamp in Burgentosh, held off against the Northerners at Bloody Ridge for three hours—"

"Four, your majesty," Seramin corrected quietly.

"That's right, four hours," the king noted with a low smile, "and recently you and your battalion defeated superior enemy forces that outnumbered you three to one in the mountains for a whole month before being injured in a battle that is being known as the riverside butcher. Did I leave anything out?"

"No, sire, I believe that's everything."

"Quiet a reputation that you have created for yourself, Seramin, in the span of less than two years. There are generals that have fought in my army all their life who cannot say as much."

"Thank you, but how… er… I mean, why do you know so much about me? Have I not proven my loyalty? Are you now turning to spy on your own officers?" He regretted the words as soon as they left his mouth.

Terin held his hands up to silence the captain. He shook his head, settling deeper into the soft cushions, eyes distant in thought. Now it was the king's turn to ask a question.

"Every man, it does not matter if he is a tiny peasant, or if he is a knightly king; we all have a reason to do the acts that we commit. I, for example, joined his Majesty Johan Fir' Anisk's army at the tender age of sixteen. I was a fool back then, seeking fame and adventure." The words struck a chord in Seramin and his heart pained at the mention of a past such as his own. "That was the reason that I fought against the orcs for six years, searching for fame and glory. Now, in my older age I realize that I was being naïve, and a fool. But that was my reason.

"Now, I ask you, Captain Seramin, a question. Why is it that you fight so courageously in the face of such danger? I know that it cannot be for any personal gain, such as money or adventures, for those men lose their courage after the first sign of bloodshed. You seem to have an inner gift, a flame that grows stronger as the darkness around this kingdom grows deeper. What drives you to kill another man?"

Seramin paused for a moment and thought. Why did he fight? He had never really thought about it before.

"My family lives only a day's ride from Thuringer, my lord. If the Northerners push through our lines they will be in harm's way. I have seen the resolve of the barbarians, and there is no place for mercy in their hearts; even for women and children. I fight to keep them safe, away from death's hand."

"Ah, I see." The king's grey eyes sparkled as he leaned forwards, skeletal hands gripping the sides of his chair. "A most admiral answer. You fight for love then?"

"Yes, your majesty, that is right."

Terin tried to give a laugh, but lapsed into a long fit of ragged coughs. Once settling down he squeezed the bridge of his nose and closed his eyes. "I caught you looking at my paintings earlier," he said without opening his eyes. "What did you think of them?"

"I was only able to see the one."

"Do you know of the story that it tells? The story of the four gods?"

"Of course. Everyone knows about it. My mother told me the tale when I was a child as a bedtime story. She told me all about the sun gods, and of Sinji and Kouja when she wanted to scare me into being good."

"True, it may just be a bedtime story, but the terror that our kingdom faces today is very much real. The army that we face is led by a king that worships Sinji, the evil goddess of blood. And I fear that if we shall lose this war terrible things will become of the kingdom, for only evil can come from worshiping Sinji. Genocide, or a mass conversion to the worship of that terrible deity.

"You do not need me warn you of the situation, our armies are being pushed back all along the front. The Northerners are fanatics; their religious beliefs allow their generals to work them into a frenzy. They have been promised eternal life after their death. How do you defeat an enemy that is not afraid of death?"

"I honestly do not know," Seramin said sadly, opening his arms in an act of hopelessness. "The enemy's army seems to be inexhaustible. For every warrior that we kill it seems that two more spring up to take his place while our forces continue to dwindle."

"It is now, I fear, that in this desperate time that my followers begin to lose hope. Just now I have heard reports of generals refusing to commit to battle. Retreating in the face of inferior enemy forces." Slouching in his seat the king seemed to wither away further, transforming into a man of even greater age than before. His head rested wearily in his hand, his breathing heavy and forced. Remaining silent Seramin looked on and waited for the king to say something. It brought despair into his heart to see his leader look this way.

"How much do you love your family?" the king finally asked.

"What?"

"I asked how much you loved your family, Captain. You did say that you fought for love, did you not?"

"I love my family with all my heart, sire," Seramin stated without hesitation.

"And how much would you sacrifice to keep them safe?"

"I would give my life for them."

The king nodded knowingly; in his younger years he too had a family before the plague had taken them.

"I called you here so that I could ask you to make a sacrifice, and a great one at that."

"I have given my answer, your grace. I would do anything to keep my family safe."

"Yes, as you have stated, but you have not yet heard of my request. I have asked other men to bear this burden and they have all turned their backs on me... no, on this empire! As the situation on the front has fallen into despair time has run out. It appears that you are the South's last hope."

Seramin's stomach churned when he heard these words. Thoughts raced to his family, happily living their lives, lives soon to be crushed if the war was lost. He could not allow it. Not in a million years could he allow his home to be overrun.

"What could one man possibly do against an entire army? I have no magic about me, and there are those that are more skilled with a blade. I'm only a captain for god's sake!" His voice turned into a broken laugh.

"Your strength is what caught my eye, Seramin. The South has one more chance to win this war, for there is a weapon that I have not yet unleashed. I fear the bitter consequences of it, but I see now that I have no choice."

"A weapon, what kind of weapon?" Seramin questioned.

The king allowed a bitter smile to spread across his face. "Look beneath your feet, and tell me what you see."

Seramin dropped his gaze to the darkness beneath the grating. Nothing stirred. It was as if a black hole, one that sucked in warmth and hope as well as light.

"I only see blackness. But I feel despair when I look into the dark."

"There is a single prisoner that is trapped below your feet. His soul is as black as the shadows that surround him, and he is more of a monster than a man, but I believe that he is the key to our victory. Sometimes the only way to defeat evil is to unleash evil yourself."

An invisible hand grabbed at Seramin's heart and gave a powerful squeeze. Looking down again he tried to imagine a prisoner that was trapped beneath his very feet, one so powerful that the king thought he could help defeat the barbarians on the North. Gathering his strength Seramin looked back into the king's eyes, which were locked onto his.

"How could this prisoner, one man, defeat all of the North?" he asked in astonishment.

"This prisoner is more powerful than you or I. He fights with inhuman strength, and unmatched zeal. In the time of his capture it took an entire army to bring him to the ground."

"Why do you need me then?"

"Because, this... monster, that is trapped beneath your feet is so powerful that he must be held in check with a magical collar. And, the only way to control the monster is to have a similar collar placed on another. This person must carry the burden of the other's soul, and his sins."

So that was the king's plan. He needed someone with true willpower to lead this prisoner like an attack dog, bringing him into battle and using him to fight the Northerners. But, the king was worried about the prisoner escaping and needed someone that had a reason to return home and so would fight to keep him in check. Someone like...

"Seramin, this could possibly win the war." The king's words broke the captain's thoughts.

"Yes, but am I strong enough? This prisoner seems to be too powerful to control. There must be someone else, another soldier that is stronger than I."

"No, no, no." Terin shook his head. "I have tried, but there is no more time. The collar will allow you to control the monster from within, and it will protect you from its rage, because you are strong enough."

Seramin thought about this, weighing the odds of the decision.

"If I say yes, I want something in return."

"Yes, of course." Terin didn't seem to be surprised by such a request.

"I want to return to my family, and never to be called back into the army. Never to be bothered again."

"Then... You agree?" Terin's eyes grew wide and sparkled excitedly.

Seramin swallowed hard. Was he really going to agree with this? "Yes."

He hadn't been in Thuringer for more than ten minutes and already the king was putting the fate of the war in his hands.

Chapter 2
Unchaining the Dog

Three days after Seramin and the king made their agreement they met again in the chamber, this time with a group of sorcerers that were preparing to perform the ritual that would infuse the collar onto Seramin's neck. Since the meeting he had drawn into his quarters and secluded himself from the world. No one bothered Seramin, and he did not emerge except to eat and to receive magic for his wounds. Some servants said that they heard fits of rage come from within the room, but others reported that their new quest stayed as quiet as a mouse.

Then, on the third day, a timid knock awoke Seramin. Ripping the door open he glared down at the shrinking servant who mumbled an excuse that the ritual was ready to begin. Seramin threw on a simple robe and limped to the king's chamber. There a small crowd of sorcerers, cabinet members, and royal guards greeted his presence. Terin sat on his throne, surrounded on all sides by the thirteen vassal lords of the empire. Seeing the savior enter brought a lighter color to his sullen face.

"He is here," he announced. "Allow the ritual to take place."

The vassal lords threw worried looks to each other. They seemed unsure of what was to take place today. Many stared hard at Seramin as if to ask, "Is he really the one?" With a slight limp and an arm in a sling he did not make an impressive-looking warrior. A look of fatigue covered the captain's face. It appeared that he had not slept at all during the three days.

The bodyguards remained in place, solid as stone. Their eyes remained the only part of their body that moved, following Seramin's path through the chamber, looking for a weakness, an opening, analyzing. Seramin noticed the leader of the guards that had led him to the king three days ago. The man gave a small nod and Seramin returned the gesture. Walking towards the king the crowd of sorcerers parted for him as if a giant hand had dipped into the river of bodies and had pulled them aside. Before the throne, in the middle of the parted sea of bodies, sat a table.

On this cloth-covered table rested the collar. Made of shining copper it was of a simple design, a single piece of metal that formed a circle with a latch on one end. There appeared to be nothing magical about the collar and it sat harmlessly on the table. Seramin limped over and looked down at the collar, sizing up the piece of metal. This was the key to power. Something seemingly worthless was to help save the empire.

One of the sorcerers brought a chair for Seramin so that he could sit while they performed the ceremony. With great reluctance he eased down into a sitting position. The act seemed to signify his submission to fate. With great care he moved his injured arm onto the left armrest. Then his right followed suit, his hand creating a claw against the wood.

With this Terin stood to his feet, wavering slightly from weakness. "Seramin, defender of freedom and strongest of the strong. You have given yourself to the service of this empire. It is with you that we will unleash a great evil against our enemy." He paused, swallowed hard and then continued, "I humbly thank you for what you are about to do. Remember that in whatever depths you fall into remember that the fate of a nation rests on your shoulders." The vassal lords threw more worried looks about themselves.

"You must relax while we chant," one of the sorcerers told him, a young man dressed in blue robes with short blond hair.

"And how am I supposed to do that?" Seramin retorted.

"Deep breaths?" the sorcerer offered with a weak smile.

"Thanks, I'll try to remember that."

The sorcerers indicated that they were ready to proceed. Terin waved for them to begin. They broke into a circle around Seramin and began to chant. A deep, haunting sound that hit Seramin in the pit of his stomach. The words rolled together into a wave of force, building strength as the spell began to form. The senior sorcerer tenderly lifted the collar from the table like a mother cradling a newborn baby for the first time, and then held it above his head, closed his eyes, and gave a quick prayer to the sun gods.

Turning to Seramin the sorcerer looked into the captain's eyes, searching for some answer; possibly to ask if this man was really strong enough. "Are you ready?"

"No"

The copper collar snapped into place with a loud click. The metal was bone cold against the captain's skin and he squirmed against the claustrophobic feeling that came over him as the collar squeezed against his airway. He tensed, waiting for bolts of lightning to wash over him, for immense spasms of pain to enter his body, but nothing happened.

Glancing nervously around the room Seramin tried to read the faces of the sorcerers. Deep in their concentration they revealed nothing. He then looked at the king, who leaned in his seat, hands folded together in prayer.

The chanting grew louder yet as the spell began to intensify. A wave of heat began to seep from the once-cold collar into Seramin's neck, flooding through his body like poison. It began filling every crevice in his body; sweat began to leap from his pores. His breathing became rapid; heart pounding in his chest as if to jump out. Something was happening; the spell had begun to take on a physical effect.

Smoke began to float out of the metal grating on the floor as a small fire erupted in the depths below. It grew larger in intensity until the entire space beneath the floor had burst into flames. Yellow and orange tongues reached through the grating, wrapping themselves around Seramin's legs and singing his clothes. The heat was unbearable; sweat poured from every single one of his sweat glands at once. Smoke filled the room, choking everyone's lungs and stinging their eyes.

Beginning to panic, Seramin attempted to get out of the chair, but long strands of chains burst out through the grating and slithered up the legs of the chair like the tentacles of a monster. Wrapping around his arms and legs the chains grasped tightly at the captain's squirming body and held him tightly in place. Screaming and fighting against the enchanted metal Seramin tried to break free, but it was useless.

Stopping their chant the sorcerers stepped backwards from the fire, their eyes wide in shock. None knew what to do; the spell had gotten out of control. The prisoner had begun to take over, he was fighting the spell!

"What is going on?" the king shouted in despair. What was happening to his favored captain? The last hope of the kingdom.

Now the pain that Seramin had at first expected from the collar began to swell in his neck. The metal burned red hot, singing his neck and burning the flesh. His screams echoed through the halls of the castle until he blacked out and lost sight of the ever-growing fire. Before he lost all consciousness Seramin thought that he heard laughter, a deep booming voice that vibrated deep within his soul.

* * * * *

Cold touched Seramin's body when he awoke. Jerking upright he grabbed at the collar that clung tightly to his body. Pulling with all of his might he tried to rip off the damned thing, but it refused to budge. Reaching his hands back to the lock he realized with dread that the lock had melted and fused itself shut. The collar was stuck permanently.

Forcing himself to relax his breathing Seramin lay back in the oversized bed that he had been sleeping in and looked around at his surroundings. The room was finely decorated with a grand red rug that covered nearly the entire floor. A wooden dresser sat in the corner, complete with a full-sized mirror. The bed frame had been carved entirely out of fine oak, ornate with carvings of flowers and small animals. A window at the far side of the room had been opened a crack by a servant, allowed a stream of chilling air to move inside.

The door suddenly opened causing Seramin to jump. A nurse dressed in a white dress with long brown hair pulled back in a bun entered the room carrying a pitcher of water.

"I see you're finally up," she noted while placing the pitcher on the desk.

30

"What happened?" Seramin asked, waiting for his heart to stop racing. His memories remained faint; he only remembered glimpses of the collar ceremony.

"You suffered some nasty burns on your legs and neck, but you should be fine."

"How long have I been in here?" he questioned, motioning at the room.

"Oh, at least two days, my dear."

"Two days?"

"Of course," she chirped happily, "it's quite common for a person who has suffered wounds such as your own to sleep for long periods of time." She walked to the door and began to close it, but then stopped and poked her head back into the room. "Oh, I almost forgot. Your clothes are on the end of the bed." She pointed. "And the king wishes to see you as soon as possible."

"Thank you."

Climbing wearily out of the bed Seramin limped over to the pile of new clothes and began to throw them on. He closely examined the burns on his legs and decided that they were minor, and would heal with minimal scarring. *What did she mean by 'nasty'? These burns aren't so bad.* Before leaving the room he stopped in front of the mirror in order to examine the collar.

It looked like a parasite that had attached to his throat. The coppery shine gave the impression of rock-hard scales of some type of snake. Ugly black burns cowered under the collar; blood mixed in with the destroyed skin. It hurt to move his neck, but Seramin shrugged his shoulders and set off to look for the king. He had suffered worse wounds before.

Terin sat alone inside the monstrous garden, alone in the sense that his bodyguards stood in rigid attention at a distance. Piles of furs wrapped the ancient king to protect from the harshness of the weather. All that could be seen of his face were the puffs of frost that erupted like steam from a pipe. Shrinking into the marble bench he gazed into the frozen pond.

Crunching of snow underfoot caught the attention of Terin. Turning around he came to face Seramin. A forced smile came to his face before turning away to look again at the pond. Not a word was said between the two men. Seramin stood uneasily, glancing between his king and the bodyguards, and then back again. After a moment of silent debate he moved to the bench and sat down. The coldness of the rock burned through the furs. Wind howled mournfully amongst the hedges; a lonely ghost of winter.

"I must apologies for the events that occurred," Terin began. "I was reassured by my sorcerers that the prisoner was weak, and that the spells would hold him in place. I did not expect for any harm to come to you."

"I seem to be just fine."

"Yes, that fact has astonished the healers for the last few days." Terin turned to the captain but no smile came to his face. "You sat in the chair, chained down as we cowered in the corner. You became incased in flames, yet they did not seem to touch you."

A cold lump fell into Seramin's stomach as he pictured himself covered in fire. He had mercifully blacked out before this could event occurred. "Were the flames and the chains part of the spell, or where they controlled by the prisoner?"

"We don't know. Very little is actually known about him: his past, his true powers, or even his real name."

"Now that this collar has been attached to my throat, what happens now?" the captain said.

Terin took a deep breath and looked down at his feet. "I have just received word that the Northerners have forced their way past the Yatze River, and are now marching forwards to Thuringer. Our armies are depleted and have little chance of stopping them."

The world came crashing down on Seramin. Breathing itself became impossible as he tried to realize what the king was saying. The Northerners had broken through the last defenses of the Southern army and were within a two-week march of the city. It was now only a matter of time before they were at his home's doorstep.

"I am afraid that you must leave at once. Without the prisoner fighting at our side I believe that all is lost. Any type of delay could cost us dearly."

"I am at your service," he managed to say, doubts flooding into his mind. Doubts about his ability, the strengths of this prisoner, and those of his countrymen.

"I know you are," the king said with tears in his eyes. "You are the last hope of this kingdom.

Chapter 3
Departure

By midday Seramin and twenty royal guards were prepared to depart. He had been given a fresh coat of chain mail along with some light plate armor that covered his legs, arms, and shoulders. A brand-new long sword hung at his side, and a collection of daggers remained concealed within his belt. All men were mounted on war horses so that they could reach the Northern army as soon as possible. The Southern forces were pulling back to positions three days' hard ride from the city where they hoped they could make another stand. It seemed doubtful, but they had no other choice.

The most curious part of the ensemble was a large stone coffin that rested on a sagging wagon pulled by a team of four horses. The coffin measured twelve feet long and five feet wide. On the sides a ring of ancient runes that Seramin could not decipher ran counterclockwise. On the top was the carving of a large warrior that had been laid to rest; he was dressed in battle armor and grasped a sword to his chest.

"This coffin is to hold the prisoner until he is needed," a sorcerer informed Seramin after he gave the stone block a questioning look. "Powerful spells will hold him at bay so that he does not escape."

"Will they now?" Seramin had lost all respect for the sorcerers after the collar ceremony.

Leaving the city Seramin twisted around in his saddle so that he could watch the white castle fade out of sight. Already small bands of soldiers could be seen outside the outermost moat, digging into the frozen ground so that they could lay a thick wall of sharpened stakes into the ground.

For two days the band traveled without incident. They would travel all day, from sunup to sundown, and took only small breaks for lunch so that the horses could rest. Few of the men spoke; they were nearing the front lines and it was known that Northern patrols could have easily snuck past the forward soldiers so that they could attack supply trains. At night no fires were built and the guards slept with their halberds close at hand.

On the third day they passed a long line of walking wounded that fled from the front. Most walked wearily without saying a word, but some stopped to warn of the fighting ahead.

"They are monsters," one exclaimed. "They continue to march through our lines no matter what casualties we inflict on them. They are not human!"

"The war is lost," another said. "We cannot defeat the Northerners, they are too strong."

The band continued moving despite the warnings that they received, but they didn't know what to say to the wounded soldiers in order to lift their spirits. As far as the eye could see was the line of wounded winding into the distance. The road had become soaked with blood, and soldiers who had died during their trek lined the road, the others too busy or tired to give them a proper burial.

At the end of the fourth day the road emptied of any other signs of human life and the band was once again alone. The terrain had become more mountainous and the road began to angle upwards, winding through heavy groups of trees and over piles of boulders. Coming to a slow-moving creek the royal guards began to cross, Seramin and the wagon protected in the middle.

The ambush had been cleverly hidden and the scouts that the royal guards had sent out had been unable to see it. Rising up from their hiding places four Northern warriors shouldered their crossbows and fired into the lead guards. The brute strength of the devices sent the metal bolts straight through the guards despite their armor. Blood flowed freely from the messy holes that had been ripped into the two lead guards and they fell dead from their horses, hitting the water with bloody splashes.

Soon the air filled with the deadly buzz of crossbow bolts as more Northerners came out from their hiding spots to fire into the trapped men. Dead royal guards fell from their mounts; some remained stuck in place, bodies shuddering as more of the deadly missiles struck home.

Charging out from the dense undergrowth warriors jumped into the frigid water, stabbing at the Southerners with spears and swords. Despite being hopelessly outnumbered and cut off the guards fought bravely with their silver halberds. Leaping down from their horses in order to present smaller targets for the crossbowmen they pulled themselves into a defensive ring and met the charge head-on.

Blood filled the creek as the Northerners were chopped down in quick succession. Being the most skilled troops of the Southern army the royal guards far surpassed the warriors in skill, but the crossbowmen, and the sheer number of the warriors soon whittled down the guards to only a few.

Fighting side by side with two of the guards Seramin parried blows at a rapid pace with his one good arm. Dodging past a thrusting spear he killed his seventh warrior with a quick slash to the neck. He then intercepted the next one, hitting him across the face and splitting his features in two. One of the guards impaled a mace-wielding warrior with his halberd before he could attack Seramin from the back, but then crumpled from a bolt to the chest.

The last remaining guard pulled a pair of daggers from his belt and threw them with a flick of his wrist, catching two of the crossbowmen positioned on the other side of the brook. He then returned his hand to the pole of his halberd and smashed a diving warrior in the face. An unseen sword from his left removed the brave guard's arm. Falling to his knees the man lost his grip on his weapon, and then was immediately impaled with three separate swords.

Ten Northerners remained, and Seramin was the last Southerner that was not dead or horribly wounded. Already exhausted from the battle he didn't know how much longer he could continue fighting with only one arm. Gripping the handle of his sword tightly he took a fighting stance and charged ahead, taking the course of action that the barbarians would least expect.

Metal rang loudly as Seramin's sword clanged against a raised shield. Swinging in a wide arc he cut out the legs from one warrior and beheaded another. Rage burned in his eyes as he lunged, impaling a third with the tip of his sword. In his death throes the impaled warrior grabbed the blade of the sword and jerked to the side, pulling the weapon from Seramin's grip.

One man with a missing eye saw the unarmed captain, and suspecting an easy target stepped up to claim his prize. With lightning-fast speed Seramin pulled a dagger out and threw it into the man's good eye socket, killing him instantly. A pair of daggers found their marks into the throats of two more warriors, leaving only four more to oppose the captain. Taking great care the four men formed a circle around Seramin, weapons at the ready. Pulling his sword from the stomach of the mortally wounded warrior Seramin waited.

They all attacked at once from different angles, hoping to catch him off balance. In a windmill of flashing blades Seramin lashed out, cutting limbs and severing tendons with amazing speed. A lone sword managed to cut into his side, but the captain quickly jumped out of the way before it could embed itself deeper into his flesh and cause more damage. The attacker, the last Northerner alive, did not live much longer as Seramin's sword buried itself deep into his chest.

The attack was over; the brook was now littered with dead bodies that floated and shifted from the current. Several of the mortally wounded warriors had managed to pull themselves from the freezing water and onto the rocky bank, but they did not have long to live. The elements would soon claim their lives.

Putting his hand to his side Seramin attempted to stop the flow of blood that poured from the wound. Thanks to the cold he did not feel any pain, but his legs were beginning to turn numb from the water. If he didn't find shelter soon the captain knew that he would quickly freeze to death. Remembering a small village that the band had seen earlier nestled between two deep valleys he set off in what he hoped was the general direction.

Completely drenched in water Seramin shivered violently as his body began to turn numb. Unable to find a secure foothold in the creek he slipped and fell, plunging into the cold, deadly water. The ground near the shore had turned to glaze ice and he had to claw his way to the trees. Tears flowed down his face as he cried from the pain in his bleeding fingertips and frozen feet. Frostbite had already begun to set onto his face, and the tender skin on his ears burned as if on fire.

Making it away from the bloody brook he stumbled through the forest. Pushing aside heavy evergreen branches laden with snow and charging through tall snowdrifts he felt himself drifting farther and farther away. He didn't have much time before death wrapped its black arms around his shoulders. Yelling loudly to himself Seramin forced himself to stay awake.

Just when everything seemed hopeless—he didn't even know if he was heading in the right direction—Seramin burst out of the forest and looked down a steep slope that led to a small village snuggled inside of a heavy blanket of snow. Smoke wisping from stone chimneys signified warmth.

The path was icy and Seramin carefully checked his foothold, but after several steps his feet pushed out from under him and he fell to the ground. Lacking friction on the steep path Seramin found himself sliding down towards the village, picking up more and more speed with every passing second. Trees whizzed by in a blur of green, slapping at his face as he flew by.

Desperately clawing at the snow Seramin tried to slow his descent, but there was nothing that he could do. Bouncing around like a rag doll he rolled and tumbled through a patch of snow-covered thorns, shredding his skin and ripping his clothes to tatters. Crashing to a stop against a lone pine tree only a few meager yards from the nearest building, Seramin felt a pop as a rib snapped under the impact.

With the wind knocked out of him the captain could only mouth silent cries until his struggling lungs were able to gasp in small amounts of air. Like a newborn baby he floundered in the snow. He only managed to whimper, but it was better than not breathing. After several minutes of sitting with his back to the tree Seramin struggled to his feet. Pain shot through his wounded chest and he clutched at the shattered rib. Dragging his feet, moving inch by inch, he shuffled to the nearest building.

When the door of the tavern flew open, revealing a battered and bruised Seramin, the people could only stare in shock. Unable to speak the captain staggered a few more steps into the tavern and then fell to his knees, grabbing at a table for support, but missing and crashing to the floor. In an instant a crowd had gathered around the fallen soldier. A pair of large men knelt down by his side and gingerly rolled him onto his back.

"What happened to you?" one of them asked, eying the scores of cuts, scrapes, and bruises that covered Seramin's body.

"A-a-a-ambushed," he managed to stammer, "by the brook."

"Northerners?" the other asked nervously. Seramin nodded.

"T-t-then I f-fell down t-t-t..." He pointed weakly outside.

"You fell down the valley?"

Another nod.

"What's going on here?" the tavern owner asked angrily as he pushed through the crowd. An old man with greying hair, he peered over the tips of his spectacles.

"It's a soldier, Kerp. He said he was ambushed up at the creek."

"A soldier?" the man asked in amazement looking down at Seramin; his expression of anger quickly melting from his face. "Quickly, bring him into the back room."

Hooking their arms around Seramin's feet and arms the two heavyset men carried him through a door in the back of the tavern and carefully laid him in a small bed that the owner pointed to. Seramin screamed when they set him down and his arms flailed around in the air.

"He looks horrible," one of the men stated.

"Yes, he is quite a mess," the owner replied as he began to examine Seramin's wounds. "He has suffered through quite an ordeal. There is a deep sword wound in his side, and it appears that he has a broken rib." He pushed on Seramin's chest and was rewarded with a piercing scream that drove the crowd back a step. "Yep, just as I suspected, a broken rib."

"Don't touch me!" the wounded man roared, and with a sudden burst of strength he pushed the tavern owner down. It looked as if the captain was about to rise to his feet, but then his eyes rolled back into his head and he fell back into the bed.

Seramin's lips had already begun to turn blue and his body was wracked with shivering. "Quickly, grab me some blankets!" the man ordered, climbing back up from the ground, dusting the dust from his jacket. Turning back to the soldier lying on the bed the man placed a hand to Seramin's forehead, feeling the fever that was beginning to rise. "Don't worry, you'll be just fine."

Seramin blacked out for the second time that week.

* * * * *

Several hours later Kerp, the tavern owner, exited the back room to be faced by a crowd of villagers that had gathered upon hearing the news. Nearly the entire village had gathered. Very few had ever seen a soldier from the king's army before.

"How is he doing?" one of the eager ones asked.

"All right, for now," Kerp shrugged his shoulders helplessly. "He is in the hands of the gods at the moment."

Kerp's daughter, a bright girl of eighteen named Shoshe, pushed her way through the crowd and moved to his side. Her golden-blond hair swished from side to side as she walked and her beautiful red lips were drawn taut. She handed a small vial to her father.

"Here are the herbs that you requested, Father."

"Thank you, Shoshe." Kerp took the vial and rubbed his tired eyes with the back of his hand. His wrinkles had grown deeper, and his hair more grey during the long hours that he had spent caring for the wounded captain.

"Has he said anything more?" his daughter asked curiously, glancing towards the closed door.

He shook his head sadly. "I'm afraid not. He was in a lot of pain before, but thankfully he is now sleeping."

"Any idea who he is?" questioned one of the men that had dragged Seramin into the back room earlier that day.

"All that I know of him is that he is a captain in the Southerner army, and that is because of the uniform that he was wearing. Strange though, was the collar that he was wearing."

"Collar?" Shoshe gave a puzzled look.

"Yes, he seems to have a metal collar attached to his neck. I tried to take it off so that he could rest better, but it is fused shut. Very strange indeed, I have never seen anything quite like it before."

"Maybe we can ask him about it later when he wakes up?" Shoshe suggested.

"Maybe," he sighed, "but we must see if he will make it through the night first. As for the rest of you," he pointed a finger at the crowd. "I want you all to leave. It is past closing time and I am exhausted."

Giving a groan of disappointment the villagers began to make their way to the door. Donning their heavy jackets they prepared themselves for the arctic blast of wind and then raced outside. Once the last man had exited the tavern Kerp gave a sigh and sank into a chair. With great care he pulled his spectacles from his eyes, folded them, placed them into his pocket, and then proceeded to bash his forehead into the table as a sigh of defeat escaped his lips. Giving a silent smile Shoshe moved behind the bar. "Would you like a sip of water, Father?"

"Yes, thank you, Shoshe," a muffled voice replied.

Placing a mug of water near her father's head Shoshe laid her chin on her folded arms; peering into Kerp's thinning hair. "Why do you think this soldier is here of all places?" she inquired once the silence became too deep for her to take.

"I don't know, and that is what scares me. I have heard stories of the war, and it seems that it is not going well for us. It is possible that the presence of this soldier means that the Northerners have pushed their way to our humble little village."

"What happens to us then?"

Kerp lifted his head from the table and gave a smile and a secretive wink that his daughter's mother had always loved. "I wouldn't worry about that. The Northerners would not bother themselves with wasting their time with such a small place as this. Besides… the South has never been defeated in war, and we will not begin now."

"There's always a first time for everything."

"Just like your mother, always thinking of the impossible."

Kerp's eyes grew distant as he pictured his long-departed wife. Three years to the week she had been taken by the plague. An incurable illness had swept through the South, killing entire villages within weeks. Once winter had settled upon the land it seemed as if the disease had died off, but then Quentin had grown ill. Using all of his powers as a healer Kerp had done his best, but she continued to grow worse with every passing day.

"Mom loved to dream."

"Yes, dream. She dreamed of peace more than anything. But there is no chance of peace in this world."

"Is that why she got so angry when you joined the army?"

"In a way. Even though I only served as a healer, which I considered a noble thing at the time, she said that I was contributing to the destruction of life. She thought that we should make peace with the orcs. With orcs of all things! If it was not for the brave soldiers, such as the one that lies in that room," he pointed to the doorway, "we would all be dead by now."

"Do you think he will live?"

"He has the fever, but I can see that the man is accustomed to pain. He will live."

The door to the tavern flew open, slamming against the wall with a loud crack that caused both of them to jump. Snow blew into the room as four heavily clothed men stomped in. They carried a makeshift assortment of weaponry: wood axes, hunting bows, and crude swords. They panted and wheezed from the taxation of their journey.

"Did you find anything?" Kerp asked anxiously.

One of them nodded a bearded, frost-covered head. "Yes, we found the area that the captain said that he was ambushed. Everyone was dead. We found twenty dead royal guards and several score of dead Northerners."

Royal guards? Kerp and Shoshe glanced at each other. Whatever reason that the captain had come to this part of the kingdom must have been very important indeed for the king's personal guards to accompany him.

"We also found something else," the man said, but then paused as if searching for the best words to use.

"Yes, what did you find?"

"There was a wagon in the brook, and on it was a large stone sarcophagus covered in runes that none of use could read."

"A sarcophagus," Shoshe thought out loud. "Was there anything in it?"

The man shook his head. "We opened it, but it was empty."

Chapter 4
Hydrib

Nightmares haunted Seramin's dreams that night. The fever had caught hold of his mind and he twisted and turned in discomfort. He relived the battles that he had fought, re-watching the horrors that he had experienced a hundred times over. His family was there too, but they were among the dead on the battlefield. His son and daughter were pierced with arrows and lay in mangled piles. His wife's throat had been slit, her blood soaking her blue dress.

"No!" he screamed jerking upright. His wounded body disagreed with the sudden jerk and he then began crying out in pain, clutching at his chest. Moments later the door swung open followed by a flickering light from a glass lantern.

"Are you all right?" a soft voice called out into the darkness.

The light from the lamp illuminated the room, revealing Shoshe as she tiptoed across the pine floorboards and knelt by Seramin's side, ignoring the roughness of the floor on her knees.

"Where am I?" Seramin asked desperately, delirious and confused. He tried to get out of the bed and began thrashing around. Shoshe grabbed him with an iron grip and threw him back onto the sheets.

"Do try to calm down," she scolded. "You are in Talron, a small village out in the mountains."

"Talron?"

"You were ambushed," the girl explained, "and you managed to make your way here after you were wounded."

The events of the previous day come back to Seramin in a mighty blur: the ambush at the brook, the coldness of the water, the fall down the side of the valley, and crashing into the tree at the bottom.

Everything after that was only blackness. Closing his eyes he groaned loudly.

"If you like I could get my father; I am a healer, but he is far better than I."

"Are there others?"

"What?"

"Are there others? Any other survivors?"

"I'm sorry, only dead bodies were found at the brook."

"What about the coffin then, do you have it?" Seramin grabbed Shoshe's arm and pulled himself close so that he could look into her frightened eyes. His breath burned her nostrils. She could feel the heat from his fever on her skin. His eyes, wild and rolling, gleamed in the light of the lamp.

"There was a sarcophagus at the brook, but I have been told that it was empty."

Seramin's heart sank, the entire world came crashing down on him in that moment. All was lost, the great weapon that the king had placed in his care was now gone, possibly in the hands of the enemy by now. The South would lose the war, and it would be his fault. He released his grip.

"Is something wrong?" Shoshe asked quietly once her breathing had returned to normal. Unable to answer he simply fell back onto the bed, his eyes glazed over and he lay staring at the ceiling. How could he possibly tell this girl what was truly bothering him?

"Why is the sarcophagus important?"

Seramin's head snapped around to look at the girl, but he then pulled his gaze away and he said nothing.

"What was in it?" Shoshe prompted.

"Please go away, I'm fine now."

Looking disappointed Shoshe climbed to her feet. "I will be in the next room if you need anything," she whispered. "Just call if you need help."

Seramin watched as she left, closing the door behind her, extinguishing the yellow light from the room. When the door closed silvery light from the moon flooded to create a pool of mercury on the floor, illuminating a large figure that had been standing next to the door.

He was wrapped in shadows. But a dark outline of a muscular body could be seen. As still as an oak tree the figure stood, staring down at Seramin, who lay frozen in place, unable to make a sound out of fear. Taking a step the man revealed himself.

He was tall with broad shoulders. A thick beard covered his face, which was set in stone with a deep scowl. His clothes were in tatters and hung loosely on his body. A silver collar clung to his neck from which a length of chain swung down to his shoulders. Once seeing the collar Seramin's breath caught in his throat. It was him! The prisoner!

"So," the man breathed heavily, "you are the one that thinks he can control me." Leaping towards the bed he placed two large hands over Seramin's neck and began to squeeze. Thrashing desperately Seramin tried to pull the hands away, but they were simply too strong. The world began to grow dark as oxygen was cut off from his brain. Then, the hands suddenly let go and Seramin was free.

Once his vision was restored he saw what had happened. The prisoner's collar had grown hot, burning his neck and forcing him to release his grip. Smoke and steam poured out from beneath the collar and the man groaned, ripping at the metal, but even he was not strong enough to remove its death grip.

"Damn it!" he hissed, throwing his arms down in disgust. "The collar holds me in check. Much to your luck."

Struggling to get his breath back Seramin backed away from the prisoner and searched for a weapon, but none were to be found so he resorted to remaining still.

"You are lucky, this time." The man pointed a threatening finger at the captain. "But I will get stronger. Then you are as good as dead!"

"You must do as I command!" Seramin's confidence began to grow. Had his life not been saved by the bond between the two collars? The prisoner scowled.

"Perhaps for a time, even I cannot deny that fact."

"How did you escape from the coffin? I thought you would only leave it when I called for you."

"It is true that I was trapped inside the coffin, but the bloodshed of the battle weakened the spells that bound me there, and then it was easy to escape. Those sorcerers of the king think that they are so smart, but in reality they are only fools."

He began to move for the door, sinking backing into the shadows.

"Where are you going?"

"I'm leaving. Don't worry, I will return," he added quickly after seeing Seramin's horrified expression. "I shall return, but there is no point in wasting my time here when you are healing."

"No, I order you to stay."

A deep laugh sounded from the prisoner's chest. Seramin's blood chilled as he recognized it from the deep laugh that he had heard in the king's chamber.

"You are not strong enough to order me around. And, as much as Terin wants to believe it, I am not some simple slave that you can force to do your bidding. I bow to no man." The door opened, outlining him and turning his body into a black shape devoid of any form.

"Can I at least have your name?"

"You may call me Hydrib."

* * * * *

"That is strange," Shoshe noted, "I've never seen anyone heal that fast before."

Seramin wondered if the collar had something to do with the sudden healing of his wounds, but he had been wearing it for several days before the attack at the brook and his shoulder and back hadn't healed at all. Both Kerp and Shoshe denied that they had anything to do with his healing. They had magical powers, but they were very limited and could not complete what Seramin had achieved overnight.

Stating that he was strong enough, Seramin climbed shakily out of the bed and began to move around the tavern. The villagers cast him sideways glances, but did little else. Their curiosity did not extend far enough to talk to this new arrival. Strangers could be dangerous in these parts and Seramin needed to be looked after, and dealt with great care. He was already associated with dead Northerners and royal guards, a black stain on his figure.

"Good to see you up and about." Shoshe beamed, seeming to have forgotten about the events of the previous night."

Seramin grunted and seated himself at the bar. The man next to him grabbed his mug and slid a few inches to the left. The captain gave the man a hard stare, but then turned his gaze back to the smiling girl who flirted back and forth behind the bar, taking orders and serving the customers their drinks. Wiping his hands dry with a towel Kerp leaned his skinny frame up next to Seramin.

"What will it be?"

"Water, please."

"Just water? Never met a soldier that didn't enjoy drowning his sorrows in a pitcher of ale before."

"Just water." Seramin began to pull his money bag from his belt but the owner held up a hand.

"Don't worry, it's on the house. Between fellow comrades in arms."

"Heh." The man that had shied away from Seramin earlier frowned with discontent. "How come he gets a free drink?"

"Because he's drinking water. Would you like a cup of water, Jurgin?"

"Hell no."

"Then shut up. I know for a fact that you still owe me from last week so pay up or get out."

Grumbling the man threw a few copper coins down then beat a hasty retreat. Scooping up the money Kerp rolled his eyes. "And he still shorts me. You would think he's trying to rob me blind."

Finishing the mug Seramin waved for Shoshe to fill it again. Upon her arrival she gave a quick glance around, and then leaned her head close to his. "So, mind telling me why you're here?"

"Yep."

"Have the Northerners broken through, will they be here soon?"

"Beats me."

"Were you returning to the front?"

"Maybe."

"You don't talk much... do you?"

"Only when I feel like it."

Giving a toss of her long hair Shoshe stood to her full height of five feet six inches and placed her hands on her hips. "Well, is there anything that you feel like talking about?"

"I need to re-supply before leaving, I could use a guide."

"Well, it's gonna cost you."

"Really? How much?"

"Information. Tell me about the war, about what's going on. Are we winning? Here in Talron nobody knows anything. It's very depressing, really."

Waving a gold coin through the air Seramin watched with amusement as Shoshe's eyes followed the glittering coin back and forth. "I'm much better at paying with this."

Snatching the coin from his hand the girl quickly pocketed the metal with the skill of a magician. Patting her pocket reassuringly she gave a guilty smile. "Where do you want to go?"

"The blacksmith and the trade store. Does there happen to be a stable nearby?"

"Yes, but I doubt anyone will sell you their horse. They're pretty valuable around here."

"I'm willing to bet that some poor farmer can be bought off easily enough. You were simple enough."

The girl scoffed at the remark.

Grabbing her coat Shoshe dismissed herself and then beckoned for Seramin to follow her. The sun had come out in full force, determined to melt the evil snow that lay glittering on the ground, openly mocking the golden orb. Birds sang sweetly, jumping from limb to limb in the old pine trees that had been planted years ago to serve as a wind breaker. Twelve-foot-tall snowdrifts clung to the north side of the trees. Children wielding coats, boots, and heavy leather mittens attacked the pile, digging deep entrenchments and laughing as they went.

Seramin stopped and watched as the kids divided into two armies, each side assaulting the other with snowballs. Every time one was hit he bowled over, laughing as they brushed the powder from their furs.

Nearly hidden by a massive snowdrift the blacksmith shop billowed puffs of black smoke from a tall stone chimney as several bodies inside worked feverishly. The pounding of hammers rang throughout the town and it was not difficult to follow the loud sound to the hidden shop. Seramin began to wonder why he had paid the girl so much to show him to the place. At the back of the shop the owner proudly displayed his wide assortment of weaponry on the wall. There were several swords, but none that appealed to Seramin.

"Your workmanship is fine, but I'm looking for something a little different."

"What do you mean by different?"

"I require a sword with a broader blade, and with a few extra inches of length." He gave the measurements to the blacksmith, and then a large sum of gold to ensure that the needed sword would be completed by the next day. The payment was more than what was required, but Seramin's money pouch was heavy from the king's good graces and he wanted to make the blacksmith happy. Happy workers moved much swifter.

"Would you like to see the monuments?" Shoshe asked eagerly as they left the shop, Seramin carefully counting the money that he had left.

"The monuments?"

"Yes, it's the place of an old temple back in the western hills."

"And why would I like to see the monuments?"

"The village's militia trains at the monuments. Your story has spread like wildfire; I'm sure they would like to meet the man that has defeated a small army of Northerners."

"Now I wouldn't say that it was an army—"

"Does it matter? Everyone needs a hero these days, and for now you are that hero. What's wrong with exaggerating a few stories?"

"The problem is that stories turn into legends, and then legends turn into myth. Legends give reason for war. Myths create war."

"If a war is just then there is no problem."

"No war is just; sometimes it's just a better alternative than not fighting. You wouldn't understand unless you have been there."

"My father fought in the Orc Wars. He doesn't see things the way you do."

"Killing orcs is one thing, killing another human is different. After a few men die on your blade you begin to rationalize your killings. You tell yourself that they aren't human, that they are only objects, then the killing becomes much easier. You watch your friends die and you tell yourself that they are just objects, not people. Their death doesn't mean anything. Soon your life turns into a dream. No one is a person anymore. No friends, no family, no enemies. Just things."

Seramin turned his back to the girl and spat into the ground. "You gonna show me to the trade shop now? I don't feel like seeing the monuments," he said without a hint of feeling in his voice.

Chapter 5
Assassins

Drunken laughter floated through the tavern as peasants swung their arms about wildly, guzzling alcohol and falling onto the floor. A fire crackled in the stone hearth as several dogs lay on the floor, basking in the inviting heat. The air stank of pipe smoke and the stench of sweat. Barmaids raced from table to table in the crowded room, yet they could not take the orders fast enough. Men resorted to shouting their drink orders across the tavern.

Sitting solemnly at the bar, nursing a mug of water, Seramin watched Shoshe as she moved about; bringing drinks to tables and taking the empty mugs back to be refilled. She joked and laughed with the men, always starting up conversations amongst them. Always smiling. Her joy brought a scowl to Seramin's face.

His heart pained to see so much happiness, a joy that he could not harvest for himself. If he could not have pleasure then no one should have it. The laughter of others was like a knife scraping against a metal rod, making him cringe away from the sound. The crackling of the fire only brought darkness to his soul. Even food turned to ash in his mouth. If he had been drinking ale Seramin was sure that it would have tasted like the water that he now sipped at.

Well after darkness descended into the valley the crowd began to thin; men stumbling home, others having to be carted away. Throwing a few coins to Kerp the captain shuffled to his room. Thoughts of Hydrib, the war, and his mission raced through his head. Lying awake he contemplated his options, of how to find the prisoner again, of how to bend the man to his will. Seramin's wounds had almost completely healed and his former strength once again flowed through his veins. By morning he would leave Talron and begin his search for the prisoner.

A small thump in the depths of the darkness caught Seramin's ears. Kerp and his young daughter had long since returned to their room to sleep, and no noise had been heard by Seramin's ears for the last hour. Taking caution he grabbed his newly purchased sword and crept to the door. Pushing the heavy oak frame aside with the toe of his boot he peeked out into the tavern's central room. Nothing moved, not a shadow, not even an animal could be seen.

With a pounding heart the captain waited, straining his ears to catch the tiniest of sounds; only the sound of his thumping heart could be heard. After several moments he pushed the door open. Waited… still nothing. Service in the army had trained Seramin to trust his senses. Something had made a noise in the tavern and he needed to find out what that was. Even the deadliest of foes could move with utter stealth. Many a man in the army had learned this the hard way.

Slowly… So slowly… Seramin leaned his head out of his room.

With a barely audible swish the assassin's blade raced towards his exposed neck. Only lightning-fast reflexes saved the captain. Snapping his head backwards he dodged the blade which buried itself deep into the wood. The captain's foot connected with the assassin's stomach throwing the man backwards before he could dislodge his weapon.

Unsheathing his sword Seramin moved to finish his attacker off, but a blur distracted him. Leaping from the shadows another assassin emerged, a flash of silver sparkling in the moonlight. A sharp pain hit Seramin's hand as the dagger nicked his skin. Surprised by the sudden attack he released his grip on his weapon and it went sliding off into the darkness. More silver shone as the other assassins revealed themselves. Once again Seramin was outnumbered, but this time he was unarmed as well. As the nearest Northerner bore down on him the captain prepared for the attack.

Metal whistled as the northerner swung his sword through the air, attempting to strike Seramin in the head. Dodging under the sword he grabbed a chair from the ground and raised it in defense. The blade sank into the wood where it lodged tightly. Pulling back an arm Seramin punched the man in the face, crushing his fragile nose.

He grabbed the sword as it fell from the other's grip, but the blade still remained lodged in the chair. The solution to the problem came when the next assassin rushed Seramin with an axe. The chair split apart as Seramin raised the sword to block the blow, then he stepped backwards as he instantly came under attack from three different directions. It took everything in Seramin's power to deflect the attacks.

Hearing the commotion Kerp opened the door to his room, stepping out into the tavern. "What in the hell is going on in here!" he demanded, but then his voice caught in his throat when he saw whom Seramin was fighting.

"Father, what is it?" Shoshe sidled up behind Kerp, rubbing the sleep from her eyes and not realizing the danger that they were in.

One of the assassins, seeing Kerp as a threat, reached into a pouch and pulled out a handful of ninja stars. Using his body as a shield Kerp jumped between his daughter and the spinning blades; he shuddered from the impact as they embed themselves into his body. One sank into his right shoulder while two others struck his chest. The fourth and final star hit him in the neck, splitting his wind pipe in a gush of blood.

"Father!" Shoshe screamed as blood from Kerp splashed onto her body while he tumbled backwards, pinning her legs against the floor. "No, no, no, no, no!" she screamed over and over again, hugging his twitching body to her chest, tears sprouting from her eyes.

Seramin was far too busy to notice the death of Kerp as he was pushed back into the bar. Flipping backwards over the barrier he narrowly avoided a swinging mace as it cracked wood into splinters. Jumping to his feet Seramin began to lash out furiously as four of the six assassins stood on the opposite side of the bar. His sword became a blur as it slashed and twisted in the air.

One of the Northerners attempted to leap up onto the bar, but Seramin cut his legs out from under him, literally. Grabbing at the torn appendages the man screamed and rolled around on the bar until he finally fell off of the edge and hit the ground; still screaming for all he was worth.

The man who had killed Korp pulled out another handful of ninja stars from his bag and threw them at Seramin. As the deadly weapons flew towards their target, the captain ducked low, barely dodging the projectiles which slammed into the rows of ale bottles. Several of them shattered, spraying the area with the foul-smelling liquid. One of the ninja stars had strayed away from the thrower's aim and struck a lamp. Fiery oil shot out, igniting the alcohol. Bottles caught fire and began to explode, turning into miniature bombs, spraying burning liquid in all directions with each explosion. One of the assassins was caught in the blast and instantly turned into a living torch.

Fire burned all around Seramin as he lay on the floor behind the bar. Glass zoomed over his back and he could smell the burning flesh of the roasting Northerner. Diving back over the bar he ducked as a multitude of glass jars exploded, ripping into his back and shredding flesh. Flipping over he landed on the ground and began to scream.

Pulling herself from under her father Shoshe began to crawl to the door, dodging through the chaos of the fight. As the jars that wounded Seramin exploded she looked in the direction of the fire. The flying glass caught her full in the face. Hands clutching at her wounded face, blood pouring from between her fingers, she screamed.

Seramin looked over; seeing the girl in her torment he felt a deep anger burning inside of him. It was a primal rage that he had not felt in a long time. Screaming, this time in fury, he climbed to his feet and rushed the assassin that had thrown the ninja stars.

In the blink of an eye the man unsheathed a pair of scimitars and halted Seramin. As they fought the fire spread quickly, moving over the walls and igniting the dry materials that made up the roof. The other assassins rushed to their leader's aid, but Seramin was moving too fast for them to react. One fell down, his throat slit, while another received a cut to his arm for his troubles. The other decided that it was better to keep his distance and not get involved.

Shoshe crawled along the floor. Blood pooled from her face to create a slick trail on the ground as she slowly moved in the direction that she believed that the door, and safety, was located. Her hand hit something; fluttering around in front of her she discovered that it was the bar. The intense heat of the fire on the other side burned the very air, but she struggled to pull herself to her feet with the help of the bar in order to move faster. The loss of blood was quickly draining her of strength and Shoshe knew that she didn't have much time left.

Both of the leader's scimitars thrust low and Seramin jumped backwards in order to prevent himself from being impaled. Unfortunately, he tripped over the unconscious assassin that he had punched earlier and fell against the bar. The scimitars came flashing in, one blocked with a desperate slash that cut through the attacker's hand; the weapon fell to the ground. The other blade knocked Seramin's sword away; it clattered on top of the bar. The assassin then tried to drive the scimitar through the captain's heart, but he reached out and snagged the man's sword arm before the blade managed to reach its mark.

"Shoshe!" he screamed desperately, his free arm reaching out for the sword. "My sword, it's on the bar!"

Despite the pain that overwhelmed her body the girl bravely felt for the sword, reaching for it with her finger tips.

"Hurry!" Seramin pleaded; he could feel the scimitar reaching closer to his heart. A few more inches and it would pierce his breast.

She felt the cold steel of the sword against her hand and pushed it in the direction of Seramin. The sword slid over the wood, pushing aside pieces of glass and burning wood as it moved… and then stopped just inches short of Seramin's outstretched hand.

Lurching to the side with all of his strength the captain managed to touch the sword with the tips of his fingers, but it was not enough. The remaining assassins stood and watched as their leader prepared to kill their target. A few more moments and everything would be over. Seramin had one last chance. "Hydrib!" he screamed as he grasped for the sword. "Help me! Help me!" The assassin chuckled. Who could possibly help this man now?

"Hydrib, I order you to help me!" the captain screamed louder still. The scimitar nicked his skin, drawing blood. Both men's arms shook with effort.

The front door burst open; a massive kick dislodged the burning piece of wood from its frame and sent it skidding across the floor. In the doorway stood Hydrib, standing tall and proud and ready for battle. On one shoulder rested a massive sword that measured nearly five feet long and half a foot wide. Black in color it seemed to suck in and absorb the light from the fire. Removing the huge sword from its perch Hydrib allowed the tip to fall so that it struck the floor, creating a loud boom. It was the sound of death knocking at the door.

The Northerners stared at the newcomer, not knowing what to expect. This warrior had the appearance of great strength, but the sword was so large he would no doubt have a difficult time maneuvering it in battle. The first to react charged Hydrib with his long sword, attempting to thrust through the new arrival's stomach.

Bringing the massive weapon to bear Hydrib knocked the attack aside, then gripped the handle of his own sword with both hands and swung horizontally. The assassin attempted to block the attack, but the momentum of the sword was too much and he was thrown backwards onto his heels when the metal clanged together. Off balance he could only watch when the black sword hit his stomach, slicing easily through the backbone and severing his body in half. The legs pounded against the floor while the upper body collapsed in a shower of blood.

Awestruck by the spectacle Seramin's attacker took his eyes off of him for a moment, just enough time for the caption to grab a broken bottle from the bar and smash it into the Northerner's eyes. Screaming the man leapt back, clutching at the bloody mass that had once been his face. Now freed Seramin found his sword and thrust, putting the blade straight through the man's throat which turned the scream into a low gurgle.

Hydrib came under attack by the two remaining assassins. Both had moved to a different side of his body in hopes of throwing him off balance with attacks from two different angles. Too experienced to fall for such a simple tactic Hydrib easily parried attack after attack with the large sword. Spinning in a series of wide circles he kept the weapon moving, using its massive weight to his advantage as he whirled faster and faster. One of the Northerners attempted to duck under the sword and move in close for the kill, but Hydrib quickly moved a hand from his massive weapon and unsheathed a short sword at his side. The smaller blade cut out the man's throat while the larger blade decapitated him on the next revolution.

Turning onto the last opponent, fire burning in his red eyes, Hydrib pressed the attack. Using the short sword for offense and the larger one for defense he pushed the man into the corner near a wall of raging fire. Sensing the danger the northerner pulled a dagger from his belt to throw at Hydrib, but the big man reached back and threw the short sword, burying it deep into the assassin's left leg. Then, turning the sword sideways he swatted the man with the dull side, crushing his fragile skull.

Seramin had ignored Hydrib as he battled the remaining assassins and rushed to Shoshe's side; she had fallen to the ground and was now beginning to grow hysterical.

"I can't see!" she screamed over and over again, clawing at her face in anguish.

"Shoshe, it's me, Seramin!" The captain took the girl in his arms.

"My face! Oh gods, I can't see." She grabbed at his jacket, her fingernails cutting into his skin underneath.

Slowly trotting over to the two Hydrib casually wiped blood from his sword. "We need to get going, more of them Northerners are coming."

"How many more?"

"A lot more." He raised an eyebrow and glanced down at Shoshe as if seeing her for the first time. "Might as well leave her, she won't last long in that condition."

Seramin's mouthed opened in shock. How could a man say such a thing! Unforgiving eyes looked out from Hydrib's face, begging Seramin to argue with him. Red anger built up in the captain's body, but he struggled to keep his emotions in check.

"No," he stated fiercely, "she's coming with us!"

"Fine." Hydrib shrugged his shoulders. "But don't expect me to carry her."

The heat from the fire grew stronger by the second. Even now Seramin could feel parts of his skin beginning to blister from the heat. Smoke invaded his lungs like a cloud, suffocating him, sending spurts of intense coughing through his lungs. Hooking his arms around Shoshe's small frame her easily lifted her up and carried her out of her burning home. In the doorway to his room her father's body had already begun to burn.

Even though blind she reached out a hand for her father, crying for help. "Father! Father! Please, don't leave him!"

Tears swelled up in Seramin's eyes, he didn't have the heart to tell Shoshe that her father was dead and that they were forced to leave his body behind to burn along with those of the evil men that had killed him. His hatred for the Northerners swelled at the same time. How much pain and death they had brought to his homeland! They were a plague among this planet that needed to be crushed.

Stepping confidently out into the night with his sword resting on his massive shoulder Hydrib led the way into the darkness. Moving as quickly as possible while pulling the blind girl behind him Seramin struggled to keep up with Hydrib, the man's shadow disappearing in the darkness. Talron grew smaller and smaller underneath them until it was only a collection of tiny doll houses. The entire way Shoshe screamed and tugged at Seramin, but he did not dare let her go.

* * * * *

Reaching the sanctuary of the tree line at the valley's crest Hydrib ducked into the wall of black. When Seramin moved behind him he stopped in his tracks, mouth falling open at what he saw.

The monuments had likely been an amazing sight a hundred years ago when they had been built, but even though they had gradually decayed over the years their beauty still remained impressive to say the least. The crumbling foundation of a small temple lay cramped between two towering oak trees that sat like bulging guards. A fountain with the carving of an angel sat in the shadows, water still bubbling up from the earth despite the winter cold; aided by a magical spell of some kind.

But, it was the sculptures that really caught the captain's eyes. There were dozens of them, each life-sized and remarkably lifelike. There were proud Southern warriors wielding broad swords and draped in heavy plate armor. There were priests in flowing robes and holding magical instruments from the gods. And there were also the sun gods and several of their Dwarfen and Elvish followers who bowed down to them in reverence. The line of sculptures faded off into the forest. Their true numbers remained a secret. For a moment Seramin regretted refusing to visit the monuments with Shoshe, but then quickly put the thought out of his head and focused at the task at hand.

Rushing into the sanctity of the ruins the captain set the girl down by the fountain and began to tend to her wounds. Cupping water in his hands he tried to wash away some of the blood, but this only caused Shoshe to scream louder. He then tore strips from his shirt so that he could bandage her face. He wrapped pieces of cloth over her eyes and forehead, leaving her nose and mouth unrestricted so that she could still breathe.

"She's being too loud; she'll give us away," Hydrib growled.

"I am not going to abandon her!"

"Well, then keep her quiet! I have seen at least forty warriors moving through the valley. They will be at the village at any moment."

Seramin turned to Shoshe, putting his hands on her shoulders.

"Shoshe, you have to be quiet."

"B-b-but it h-h-hurts."

"I know it hurts, but I need you to try to stay quiet."

"Father…" she cried pressing her hands to her face.

"He's gone, Shoshe." It was all Seramin could say at the moment. She began to cry and he hugged her to his body.

"Shut her up," Hydrib hissed, "the Northerners are at the village!"

Running to Hydrib's side the captain followed the larger man's gaze. One by one small pinpricks of light burst through the night. The dry kindling of the houses quickly burst into flames as torches where thrust through windows and doors. Within moments all of Talron was bathed in flames.

Looking out to the burning community Seramin watched as tiny ant-like figures swarmed about. The screams of the villagers struck Seramin's ears sharply; cut down without mercy. Commands rang out as the barbarians moved about the village methodically butchering any that lived and burning every structure to the ground.

"They didn't stand a chance," Seramin growled, clutching a hand into a tight fist.

"Just the odds the Northerners like. Easy victory without a fight."

Shoshe began to cry out again and Seramin left the prisoner to move to her side.

"Don't leave me." Shoshe sobbed as she clutched at the captain.

"I won't leave you."

"Swear it."

"I swear."

"Don't let them get me, they're coming for me!"

"The Northerners won't get you. Me and Hydrib will fight them for you."

"H-Hydrib? W-who is Hydrib?" she stammered.

"A friend."

"I am nobody's friend," growled the prisoner; he moved over to the pair. A sneer covered his face; the darkness twisted his features into a grotesque picture. "Monsters don't have any friends."

Distant shouts grew louder as Northerner sorcerers caught the scent of the three survivors. A look of fear crossed Seramin's face and Shoshe, lying on the ground, clutched terrified at his leg. Hybrid smiled evilly.

"What are you afraid of? There are only forty of them."

Was this man crazy?

"You cannot possibly take on forty warriors alone."

"Of course not, I have you."

Moving into the darkness Hybrid found a position where he could hide and wait for the attack to come. Seramin grabbed Shoshe by the shoulders and lifted the girl to her feet.

"Shoshe, listen to me. More Northerners are coming; I need to find a place to hide you."

"Northerners? We must run!" She tried to break away from his iron grip.

"There is no time." He cringed from his lacerated back before continuing, "Don't worry, you will be all right."

Moving Shoshe to the old and crumbling steps of the monument

Seramin squinted in the darkness and saw that the ground underneath had eroded away to create a small cubbyhole just big enough for the girl to fit in. Guiding her in with his arms the captain gave a few more words of encouragement before running to prepare for the attack. Shoshe whimpered softly as he left. The eternal darkness of her blind eyes wrapped around her. She was more alone than she had ever been in her life.

Using a following spell the sorcerers easily tracked Hydrib, Seramin, and Shoshe up the side of the valley to the monuments. The heat trails from their bodies glowed a dull red amongst the cold snow. Reaching the tangle of trees and stone the sorcerers pointed towards their hiding places. The leader of the band nodded, and then ordered his men forwards.

Moving as silently as possible the warriors crept into the blackness. They moved much slower once the statues came into view. In the dark they appeared to be real at a glance and the men were continually twitching and drawing their arms when a statue "jumped" out at them. Several of the Northerners carried crossbows similar to those that had killed many of the royal guards at the brook two days ago. They held the weapons to their shoulders, ready to fire at the first sign of movement.

Sitting in the darkness next to the statue of a crying woman Seramin took careful note of these men. With great care he pulled a dagger out and tested its weight in his hand. He would have to act quickly in order to take out the crossbowmen.

Just as he was about to step out and throw the dagger at the nearest target the crunch of a boot stepping through the snow sent Seramin scurrying back to his hiding place. The barbarians had spread out and were now carefully searching through the monuments. A lone warrior walked through the rows of statues, checking behind each one to make sure that no one hid behind it.

Coming to the crying woman he tipped his head behind the stone… and in a silver flash his head was rolling about the ground sending small spurts of red onto the white covering. Hearing the clang of Seramin's sword the crossbow men turned, looking for the source of the noise. A blade cut into the nearest's throat, killing instantly. The rest jumped, catching sight of the captain as he charged; one hand held his sword high while the other reached for another dagger.

One man was able to get a shot off, but he had rushed and his aim was slightly high. The bolt flew at Seramin's head, but he jerked it out of the way, and moments later another dagger had found its mark. Now the other five crossbowmen were bringing their weapons into position. Seramin could not dodge five bolts at once.

The world turned to slow motion as Seramin watched one of the crossbows fire; the crossbowman had panicked and the bolt sailed harmlessly to the left. The next shot was better. Bending his body so that his back became parallel to the ground the captain dodged the bolt while sliding a dagger from his boot. With a flick of his wrist he threw the blade underhand and dove behind a wide oak tree as two bolts dug deep into the hard wood; the third never left the crossbow for its user was now dead.

Slipping in the snow Seramin struggled to get back to his feet. He saw a flash of silver and black out of the corner of his eye just in time to put his sword above his head and prevent a large war axe from splitting his skull. Dropping to his knee Seramin sliced the man across the belly, dropping him to the ground. Giving a cry the Northerner attempted to rise back to his feet but Seramin smashed him in the face with the hilt of his sword.

Hearing the commotion the rest of the band turned and began to sprint towards Seramin. A group of ten raced from the ruins of the temple, but a dark shape stepped out from behind a tree and one of the men flipped over backwards as a large arm caught him across the neck. Hybrid came at the warriors with his sword flying. Using the oversized weapon like a club he batted weapons to the side, crushed bone, and snapped limbs like twigs. The Northerners fell back in surprise.

Seramin broke into a run. Two usable crossbows lay on the ground and he needed to get to them before an enemy warrior did. Lurching through the high snow he could see his goal in sight. Sitting on the ground beside the feet of the three living crossbowmen were the weapons. Crossbows were very powerful, and capable of penetrating plate armor at long ranges, but they were cumbersome weapons and took a great deal of effort to reload. The crossbowmen were in the process of doing this and they had no chance.

Seramin quickly cut down those remaining with a sweep of his sword, and then dropped to one knee. Snatching one of the crossbows from the snow he raised it to his shoulder and took aim at the nearest Northerner. The man wore light plate armor and a coat of chain mail beneath his leather clothes, but this mattered little at such a close range. The bolt easily penetrated through the first layer of armor, passed through his body, went through the next layer of metal and continued its flight off into the night. Throwing the empty crossbow down Seramin searched for the other.

Hybrid was now surrounded by warriors. They formed a ring around him and rushed from all sides, but he was now in a primal rage and his sword felt as light as a feather. Men screamed as they were cut down by the savagery of his attacks. A statue was cut into several pieces as it became caught between Hydrib and a Northerner with a halberd as they hacked away at each other, both using the stone warrior as a shield. Once it had been reduced to ruble the barbarian succumbed to Hydrib's blade. Turning around he searched for more targets; there were plenty to choose from. His face broke out in a grin at the sight.

Eyeing another target Seramin took aim with the second crossbow; a figure in a black robe. He was walking slowly towards Seramin and appeared oblivious to the weapon that he held in his hands. The captain paused for a moment, trying to figure out what this man was thinking, but then came to his senses and fired.

Raising a hand the sorcerer muttered the spell that would protect him from the projectile. His body grew weak as the spell took hold of him, and began draining him of his strength. The bolt struck his chest, but then passed harmlessly through his body. An ugly gash appeared in the robe as the pointed tip pierced it, but the sorcerer's body had become matterless for a brief second and the bolt could cause no damage to him for he was technically not there. Placing his hands together in front of his body to form a circle the sorcerer began chanting another spell. A small orb of blue light began to shine between his fingertips.

The captain's eyes grew wide as he realized who the man was. Seramin had encountered several sorcerers in battle, and they proved to be very dangerous enemies indeed. Their powerful offensive spells were strong enough to wipe out entire squadrons of soldiers in a single moment. They proved to be a match even for the well-trained wizards of the South. Throwing the crossbow aside Seramin dived to the ground as the sorcerer released the orb. Burning a fiery path through the air it slammed into a tree which promptly exploded.

Splinters of wood flew in all directions as the trunk burst open. Frozen water that had been trapped in the tree instantly turned to steam and hissed loudly as it escaped. The large hole in the base of the trunk was more than the tree could take. Screeching a horrible death cry the large tree began to topple over.

Spitting snow from his mouth Seramin looked up in time to see that a very large tree was about to fall on him. Rolling over he put his arms up to protect his head as a puzzle of limbs and branches fell about him, digging into the frozen earth on impact.

Thinking that he had trapped his enemy the sorcerer walked slowly to the tree, preparing another spell in order to finish the captain off. As he neared the tangle of wood he searched for the body among the branches. The sorcerer barely managed to dodge to the side as Seramin's sword hissed through the air, cutting through branches and nearly taking the sorcerer's head off. Releasing the spell prematurely the sorcerer threw a handful of bright red sparks which quickly ignited the tree branches on impact.

The tips of his clothes on fire, hair singed, Seramin jumped out from the scorched tree with his sword swinging wildly. Pulling his own sword from its scabbard the sorcerer accepted Seramin's melee attack. Sorcerers and wizards were well trained in the art of a sword because it was difficult to cast a spell while in close quarters with an enemy soldier. That was why they were so dangerous; their combination of spells and fine swordsmanship allowed sorcerers to attack in a wide variety of ways, sometimes even combining their attacks.

Warriors joined the fray as Seramin and the sorcerer fought each other. Picking up a discarded sword from the ground the captain fought with two weapons, one against the sorcerer, and the other against the warriors that tried to stab him in the back.

He soon fell into a steady rhythm. Fending off the black-robed figure with his left hand Seramin felt the sword in his right bite into flesh numerous times. Blood ran freely onto the ground, but more warriors came to replace those that he killed.

Impaling a warrior in the stomach Hybrid threw him to the side as he freed his sword from the burdensome weight. A great number of the northerners lay dead at his feet. They had charged him with reckless abandon, but he had cut them down with cold efficiency.

He felt the presence of the second sorcerer before seeing him, but when Hybrid turned to meet this new attacker he was struck hard in the chest with a spell. Flung off of his feet he flew through the air and crashed into a statue, breaking off large chunks of stone as he hit. Sitting on the ground Hybrid coughed up blood, his vision blurred and his mind scrambled. When he was finally able to register what had happened the sorcerer was nearly atop him, sword gripped in both hands and prepared to deliver the killing blow.

"For Sinji!" the man screamed before plunging the sword down at Hybrid's heart.

It never reached its target; grabbing the head of the broken statue Hybrid blocked the sword in a shower of stone chips and then smashed in the sorcerer's knee an instant later. It broke with a satisfying pop and reversed direction. Snatching up his own sword Hybrid grabbed the Northerner's collar and pulled him towards his body, driving the man through the thick blade. It caught on the sorcerer's ribs and his body writhed as Hybrid slowly forced the blade through; it finally erupted from the man's back with a loud crack.

The sorcerer's head flopped backwards, blood pooling from his mouth. "It does not matter," he wheezed, "Sinji will become victorious. She will consume your soul with the fires of hell." The last word came as a garbled yelp as Hybrid twisted the sword still deeper.

"Not if I send you to hell first." Blood spat from the prisoner's mouth onto the sorcerer's face as he spoke.

Twisting his body around Hybrid swung the sword, and the sorcerer that was still attached to it, into the remains of the broken statue. It broke into powder and the Northerner became crushed in the process.

Seramin and the sorcerer broke apart for a moment of rest. The last of the warriors had fallen to the captain's swords and only the two combatants remained.

"You, fight well for a Southerner," the sorcerer gasped between deep breaths.

"And you for a Northerner."

"Sinji warned me that I would fight skilled warriors in the warmer climates, but I never thought I would meet someone such as you on the battlefield!"

"To hell with you and your dark goddess," Seramin spat. "You and your people deserve worse than death for what you have done to my land. All for a damn goddess that demands death and blood."

"You have never experienced the power that evil can bring to a man." The sorcerer curled his hand into a fist. "The power is incredible! And you will have it too once the goddess comes to power!"

Giving a low growl Seramin charged the Northerner, determined to kill him. In a fury of swords the two twisted and danced in a beautiful and deadly display of swordplay. Their blades were almost too fast to watch. For several moments it appeared that neither would achieve the upper hand, but then the Northerner managed to summon a smell amidst the sword fight and blinded Seramin with a sudden flash of light. Grabbing his eyes Seramin lost his grip on one of his swords while tripping over a corpse, falling onto his back.

Shouting with glee the sorcerer stood above Seramin and began to cast a spell, determined to finish this enemy off once and for all. Still blinded, but able to hear the chant, the captain slashed out blindly, catching the Northerner in the leg. The blow caused the man to jerk his outstretched hands upwards and to release the lightning spell that he had just finished summoning.

The supercharged bolt of lightning struck a large limb overhead, cracking it in half. Unable to stay upright any longer, but not completely broken through, the limb swung downwards like a pendulum. Catching the sorcerer in the chest the limb launched him thirty feet before snapping off and flying away in the same direction. Only a handful of twigs had even touched Seramin, and all that he suffered was a small scratch on his cheek, while the sorcerer wouldn't be doing much of anything soon.

Once his eyes had cleared from the spell Seramin slowly sat upright and took note of the monuments, now littered with dead bodies. Sitting on a log was Hybrid, his chin resting in the palm of one hand while the other strummed on the wooden seat.

"You could have helped me!" Seramin shouted angrily.

"You never asked for my help," Hybrid answered innocently opening his arms wide, "and besides, the sorcerer had almost ridden me of your presence."

Chapter 6
Forces of Darkness

Defnork was the mightiest fortress in the Southern kingdom. Positioned four miles south of the Yatze River the fortress overlooked the main road that led to Thuringer. On either side of the fortress steep cliff faces stood tall, impassable for a hundred miles in both directions. Years of hard labor had been required to cut through the rock so that a road could be built for easier trading in the southern reaches of the kingdom. Wedged tightly between the cliffs Defnork guarded the entrance of the road.

Made of giant slabs of granite the walls were virtually impenetrable and rose to a towering height of sixty feet. On either side of the wall a large, one-hundred-foot-tall guard tower frowned down upon any invaders that dared to attack the fortress. Atop the towers sat heavy ballista that could launch a bolt one hundred yards away. Numerous firing slits had been built into the side of the wall so that archers could shoot at enemy warriors while remaining safe, or so that spearmen could attack anyone crazy enough to attempt to scale the wall with ladders.

Behind the wall sat four heavy catapults that seemed out of place for defense, but they could be loaded with dozens of small rocks. When fired simultaneously the catapults could create a rainstorm of rocks that would come crashing down, cracking bones and crushing skulls. Mortar pits lined the wall; small holes about the width of men, perfectly circular in shape and running down the interior of the wall before curving outwards and ended in a second opening near the bottom of the wall. Heavy stone balls could be rolled into the hole where they would fall down the wall and launch themselves horizontally at the bottom, shattering ladders and taking out scores of warriors as they lined themselves up, ready to climb.

The walls were scorched black with soot and numerous cracks and chips ran up and down its length. The gate now stood broken, split in half and lying on its side giving the front of the fortress the appearance of a toothless, gaping skull. Fires burned in one of the towers as the wooden support beams inside blazed, a column of night-black smoke drifted into the air.

Dead lay strewn about the fortress in large piles; rivers of blood ran heavy with the thousands of dead Northerners that cringed in their last dying acts. Beneath the wall the ground was cluttered with mountains of dead, arrows protruding from many of their bodies. Broken ladders and battering rams peeked out from the ocean of corpses. The road was now blocked off by a broken siege tower; rocks had ripped large holes into its soft underbelly and small sections had caught fire.

Long columns of barbarians marched through the open gate, moving even deeper into Southern territory as their conquest came ever closer to completion. Survivors of the bloody siege mounted the walls, manning the ballista and catapults that had so devastated their forces for the last four nights. Some were at work clearing the fortress; piling corpses, Northern and Southern alike, in two long piles that lined the road that cut through the center of the fortress. Some piles stood eight feet tall and grew higher by the minute. At the end of the day horse-drawn wagons would come so that the bodies could be loaded and dumped away from the area.

Standing atop the wall Pouja, the king of the Northerners and the leader of the great army, frowned as he watched his men march south. The fortress had taken longer to siege than had been expected. The Southerners had been given four days in order to prepare for his next attack, and, following their doctrine to the letter, they would make his forces pay dearly for each yard of land. Not only had the Southerners been given time to prepare, but a large section of his forces had been killed, and the remainder was now physically and mentally drained. Some could barely walk in a straight line. The harsh words and blows from their captains were all that kept the barbarians moving.

"Damn the Southerners!" he growled pounding his fist into the hard stone that had cost his magnificent army four days and nearly four thousand of his men's lives, leaving less than eight thousand to take over Thuringer. Pouja knew that defeating the Southerners wouldn't come easily, but he hadn't expected it to be this difficult either!

A lone rider appeared in the distance, pushing his mount as fast as the animal could move. The king watched with pursed lips as the man pushed his way through the tired warriors and moved through the gate. Dismounting from the horse he gave the reins to a servant and rested his tired legs.

"What news from the front?" a warrior cried from the ramparts. All stopped their work and looked at the rider, eager to learn of any news.

"The Southerners are running out of room to run!" the rider called out happily, which brought a series of cheers from the rest of the men.

Moving down the steps of the wall Pouja strode over to the rider, who gave a quick solute.

"Lord Pouja," he said respectfully.

"Colonel Zigmon," Pouja said in a cold voice, "you bring news from the front?"

"Ay sir, I do." He cast his eyes around to make sure that no one was around and then leaned in close to whisper to the king, "Perhaps we should speak in private, sire."

Nodding his head in agreement the king led the way to his private chambers in a flash of a wolf-skin cape and a tingling of mail against jet-black plate armor. Moving to the nearest building that sat inside of the fortress Pouja pushed the door open and stepped inside. The dead Southerners that had been slaughtered while taking refuge inside the building had already been removed, but bloodstains still covered the walls and floor.

Leading the way up a flight of stairs to the third floor Pouja moved into his chambers. The colonel gave himself a moment to take in the surroundings. This had been the private chambers of the old Southern commander of the fort and was lavishly decorated with an oversized bed complete with large, cushy pillows, bright red curtains that covered a large glass window, and a massive desk that cowered in the corner.

The only item not native to the décor was a small shrine that Northern priests had built in the center of the room. A grey stone table measuring six feet long and three feet wide sat on the floor; rising up behind it a tall stone engraving of the dark goddess herself. A coiled serpent with hooked fangs glared out at the two men with its ruby eyes. Drooping candles covered the altar, which showed that it had been used recently.

"We are alone, Zigmon, what news do you bring?" Pouja's words were laced with venom. His mood had grown considerably worse since the siege had begun and now it had become almost dangerous to speak with him. Two sergeants had already lost their heads because of their leader's foul mood.

"The defenders of the fortress were able to buy their army enough time in order to regroup. As we speak they are massing their forces about twenty miles south. Scouts reported seeing several thousand infantry and heavy horse."

"That is nothing that we cannot handle, especially with the favor of Sinji on our soldiers."

"True, my lord." Zigmon chose his words carefully. "But the terrain is difficult and there are several small forts that guard important roads that lead to the central kingdom. The Southerners will most likely use the terrain to slow us down as they have done before."

"Have these pigs no courage to meet our forces in open battle?" Pouja raged pacing the floor. "I am tired of playing these games. The Southerners sit in their fortresses or in the mountains while we are forced to rout them out. It is costly, and it takes time! Something we have very little of."

"Perhaps we can call a halt to our troops' advance and lure the Southerners out into open battle?" Suggested the colonel.

"Stop our march to Thuringer, the very heart and soul of the Southerners' spirit? Have you lost faith in our cause?" The king nearly screamed the words.

"N-no, my lord. Of c-course not," Zigmon stammered, his body wracked with fear. "I am simply saying that perhaps we should try to persuade the enemy to come onto the offensive."

"Sinji demands that we take the city as soon as possible. Any further delays are unacceptable. The army gets no rest. We march on. One more defeat and the Southern army will have nowhere to go. Thuringer will fall."

Squeezing his gauntlet into a massive fist the king began to pace about the floor. Already the thought of victory was in his mind. Years of bloody battles and difficult campaigns had now boiled down to this; victory was within Pouja's grasp. He just needed to reach out and grab it.

"No, they will not fight; we must keep pushing until they break. We shall send our main force to the east so that the Southern army will shift to meet them. We will also send a smaller force to the west. They will take control of the surrounding fortresses. When this is accomplished, the Southerners will be flanked and forced to withdraw to Thuringer. With the fortresses in our control the enemy will be unable to attack us."

"What of the men's strength? Some of them are dying while on the march."

"That is a minor matter. The greater good is more important than a few individuals' lives."

Zigmond froze, not knowing if he had heard his leader correctly. Did the "individuals" include him as well? He did not know much about the common warrior's thoughts, but he was unwilling to die for some goddess that he had never laid eyes on.

"You are dismissed, Colonel."

"Yes, yes of course." Giving a low bow Zigmond quickly left the room. He gave a sigh of relief once out of the king's hearing.

Kneeling in front of the shrine Pouja pulled a knife out and held it in his outstretched hands to the image of Sinji.

"Sinji, dark goddess of death and blood," he prayed, "I offer myself to you fully. Your power is great, and the taste that you have given me has brought me closer to fulfilling your wishes."

Holding the knife to his hands Pouja sliced the blade deep into the palm of his left hand, barely wincing as a steady stream of blood began to flow. Squeezing his hand into a fist he allowed the crimson liquid to fall onto the shrine.

"Please accept this sacrifice for failing you. I have not yet released you from your prison, nor have I defeated the evil Southerners, but victory is close at hand."

The red eyes of the statue began to burn with a bright light.

Pouja.

A low voice hissed from inside the shrine.

"I am here, my mistress." The king bowed his head in reverence.

The sssouthernersss are near defeat, yet they grow ssstronger with every passssing day.

"They are no match for me. They will be defeated."

Perhapsss. But I will not be denied again. I mussst intervene.

Pouja's head snapped up in surprise. "You will risk—"

Fool! the goddess shrieked, cutting off his words. *Do not quessssstion me! Your attack againssst the captain and the prisssoner hasss already failed, and I will not accept another failure!*

How could she have possibly known about that before he even did? And how could the captain from the Southern kingdom have escaped the force that he had sent down to kill him, which measured nearly one hundred strong? Pouja wanted to tremble with fear, but kept his composure. To show weakness in front of Sinji would be foolish.

"I don't understand, how could the captain have defeated my men?"

The prisssoner hasss been releasssed from hisss prissson. The two are linked and the captain isss drawing ssstrength from thisss weapon.

Pouja shook his head in dismay. "How can one man be so powerful?"

That isss of no importance to you, Pouja; you mussst find a way to kill thisss threat. The prisssoner can be defeated, but do not underesssstimate him. He isss ssstronger than you think.

Did he hear a hint of fear in the goddess's voice?

"Yes, forgive me." He lowered his head in submission. It was not wise to question Sinji.

I need a sssacrifice. Find me a young girl. Any will do.

"Of course, great Sinji."

Chapter 7
Through the Mountains

Sunlight filtered through the heavy canopy of trees that layered the mountainside. Snow and ice clung to the ground, desperate to stay safe from the savage winds that frequently blew through the area during the night. Morning birds chirped merrily, not sensing the bloody massacre that had taken place no more than a day's walk away. A thin sliver of white smoke could still be seen; a final marker for Talron's death.

Shoshe remained silent and limp in Seramin's hands. The events of the previous night had left her drained of energy and had stolen away her will to fight. The death of her father had been particularly hard on her; tears would have sprouted from her eyes if they had not been destroyed by flying glass. Trudging behind the captain Hydrib limped slightly from several superficial wounds that he had received in the battle at the monuments. His sword was slung over his shoulder yet he never stumbled under the heavy weight. To add to his dangerous appearance the man had raided the bodies of the dead warriors and had increased his armament.

A pair of short swords hung on either side of his waist, along with an assortment of knives, hatchets, throwing stars, and throwing pins that were tucked into his belt. Inside of his boot Hydrib had placed yet another dagger, and strapped to his back was a long sword. Seramin was amazed that the man could even move under such weight, let alone fight with all of it. But, there was more to Hybrid that he knew, and the prisoner had already proven that he was much more powerful than the average man. The giant sword that he wielded so effortlessly was proof enough of his strength.

By midday the group had ascended the first peak of a long line of green-and-white-speckled mountains that lay before them. Seramin knew of several fortresses that the Southern kingdom had built years ago in order to protect the mountain passes, and he hoped that one of them would be able to provide shelter, and to take care of Shoshe. They were unsure of the number of warriors that were following them, but Seramin didn't want to wait to find out.

A small brook opened out in front of them, and the captain had a sudden flashback of the killing of the royal guards, but the area seemed secure enough and he called for a break. He set Shoshe down on the ground on which she simply collapsed, unwilling to even lift herself.

"Pitiful," Hydrib muttered. Seramin ignored the comment.

Breaking open his pack he tossed a piece of salted park at the prisoner, who snatched the meat out of the air with one hand and greedily gulped it down. Seramin then handed a piece to Shoshe, but she refused the food.

"Come on, you must eat."

"I'm not hungry."

"But you must keep up your strength."

"I said I don't want to eat."

"Waste of food," Hydrib remarked. "I'll take it if she doesn't want any."

Seramin glared at the man, then put the meat back into his pouch. He would try again later.

"Why do you have to do that?" Seramin turned to face the prisoner. The captain's face turned red and his fists balled at his side.

"Do what?"

"Cut her down; treat her like that."

"It's nothing personal; it's just the way I am."

"What? What kind of excuse is that? There must be some good inside of that black heart of yours."

Hydrib shrugged. "Maybe, but I haven't seen it. I'll let you know if I find any."

Hydrib placed a hand on the hilt of a short sword, waiting for Seramin to retaliate. Seramin wanted nothing better than to wipe the evil grin from the man's face. Holding his ground the captain fingered his own weapon as well.

"I'm curious," Hydrib continued casually, "how did Terin choose you to wear that collar? Did he see some sort of inner strength? Unproven bravery? Or maybe he had no other choice?"

"I was strong enough to summon you last night!" Seramin spat back.

"Oh, really?" The prisoner's eyebrows shot upwards. "You call that strength? I call it desperation. If a man isn't strong enough to fight for himself then he isn't worth saving at all. A pity the collar forced me to return and save your worthless life."

"Don't dare impugn my honor!"

"There is no such thing as honor! It's an allusion that men make. They try to find a speck of light in the darkness of war. And I tell you now, Seramin, that there is no light in war. War is about killing, nothing more, nothing less."

"Odd words from a man that is so good at it," the captain mocked.

Hydrib scowled in anger. "I do not kill for the sport, we all have our reasons."

A stick snapped; both men drew their weapons and took a fighting stance, waiting for the attack of Northern warriors to come, but everything remained still. Shoshe's head twisted in every which way, trying to locate the direction of the noise. A whimper began to rise from her throat. Hydrib, taking care with his footing, stepped out into the brook and began to wade across.

"What are you doing?" Seramin hissed. His voice filled with the growing fear in his stomach.

Hydrib stopped in the middle of the moving water to look back at the captain. "To find out who's out there." With that, the prisoner crossed over the brook and disappeared into the wall of trees on the other side.

"Seramin?" Shoshe whispered; her hand waved in the air as she searched him out.

"I'm here." He grabbed her hand and crouched by her side. His eyes searched for any signs of an attacker.

"What is happening?"

"I don't know, Shoshe, it could be an animal."

He felt the enemy's presence before anything else. Spinning around Seramin jerked his head up to look at a towering man dressed from head to foot in a dirty brown robe. The man stood at least six feet tall and was built heavy with broad shoulders. His face was hidden by his hood which placed a black shadow where his features should have been. Above his head he held a heavy war axe in his hands, preparing to drive the heavy blade into Seramin. Rolling to the side the captain narrowly missed the weapon as it slammed into the ground, burying deep into the rock-hard dirt. Shoshe fell over and rolled away from the danger, screaming as she went. Yanking the axe from the ground the figure looked at both of his opponents, then settled on Seramin for he was the real threat.

Bringing his swords into the air Seramin used both to block the axe. His hands stung from the force of the weapon which drove him backwards. Unable to move away from the attacker Seramin desperately blocked the axe again and again; each time his blades met with the heavy weapon his hands burned from the impact. The figure sensed the effect that his attacks were having on the captain and increased his efforts, determined to knock the swords from his hands.

The axe succeeded in throwing one of Seramin's blades from his hands; the figure raised the axe back as far as he could, preparing for the killing blow. At the last possible second Seramin rolled to the right, dodging the axe as it thudded against the ground, and swiped the man's leg with his remaining sword. Digging deep into the flesh the sword drew blood which sprayed from the wound. Roaring in pain the axe-wielding man stumbled backwards, giving Seramin the time that he needed to get back to his feet.

They stood their ground and eyed each other, waiting for the other to make the first move. The hooded figure moved first. Swinging the axe horizontally he hoped to take off Seramin's head, but by tipping his body backwards Seramin dodged the axe as it missed his chin by inches. The next attack connected with the second sword and it was sent flying over the brook where it hit the water and disappeared in a fountain of bubbles.

"Uh-oh."

Spying an old log on the ground Seramin picked up the makeshift weapon and turned to face the man. The figure only laughed, a horrible garbled sound that sounded as if he was choking on a chicken bone that had logged in his throat.

The axe hit the ground for the third time as Seramin moved about nimbly. Cursing his luck the man attempted to pull the axe out from the ground. Seramin was faster. Jumping to the man's right he swung the log with all of his force. Fortunately, the log connected squarely between the man's shoulder blades and forced him away from his great axe. Unfortunately, the log was rotten and broke apart in half, leaving Seramin defenseless yet again.

That left only one option. Jumping at the man with his fists flying Seramin moved in close. His right connected squarely with the man's stomach; it felt like punching a tree trunk. Seramin then launched a left across the figure's chin. He pulled back nursing a sore hand. Giving another laugh the man punched Seramin, knocking him flat on his back. Stars erupted in his vision as the massive fist drove him to the ground. The whole world spun crazily, the skyline and trees tilted and swayed. *That's strange.*

When Seramin's mind cleared he was looking up at the man again as he stood over him. Something was in his hands. "Uh-oh."

It was a boulder twice the size of the captain's head that had been pulled from the ground by the man's tree-trunk arms. Groaning with effort the man slammed the rock down into the ground as Seramin somersaulted backwards. At that moment Hydrib decided to enter the fight. A log connected squarely with the man's head, this one being slightly larger than the one that Seramin had used, and this one wasn't rotten either.

"It was about time that you showed up!"

Hydrib just shrugged his shoulders and tossed the log aside. Groaning loudly the figure in the brown robe rolled about the ground and grabbed his wounded head in agony. Seramin held his head between his hands, climbing gingerly to his feet.

"That's twice that you owe me." Hydrib held up two fingers.

"Put it on my tab."

Once getting his bearings Seramin checked on Shoshe to make sure that she was all right, and then focused his attention on the hooded man that lay prone on the ground. The dirty robes and crude axe proved that this man was not a Northerner, but Seramin figured that it was not coincidence that he had been attacked.

"Why did you attack me?" Seramin demanded angrily, giving the man a kick in the ribs.

"Arg! You's hat in my home come!"

"How were we supposed to know we were in your home? We didn't mean you any harm."

"Ahh! You's humans all same. You's kill me sure."

"You humans?" Seramin looked questionably at Hydrib, who just shrugged in confusion.

"Stand up," he ordered, giving another swift kick.

"Fine! I's get up now."

Rolling to his feet the figure reached up to remove his hood.

"Orc!" Seramin cried when he saw what was standing in front of him.

Covered in green skin the orc's face was crunched together like a pig's; two tusks sprouted from his lower mouth and curved upwards, stained yellow with age. Two leathery ears stood on either side of his head and a dirty mop of black hair filled with leaves and sticks fell over a pair of red eyes. Golden earrings filled one ear and a long, nasty scar ran from the orc's left eye to his lower chin.

Shoshe gasped when she heard Seramin. All people had heard tails of the hordes of orcs that lived in the eastern mountains. Vicious and barbarous beasts that loved nothing better than to pillage defenseless towns and kill all that lay before them. Orcs were the subject of many scary stories that parents told their children before tucking them in bed.

"How does a single orc make his home this far west?" Hydrib asked, more in curiosity than anger.

"I's not live with ta others. They's not like me's anymore."

"You mean you're an outcast."

"Ay, now's I's live alone. Here's me's home!"

"Why were you thrown from your home?" Seramin asked.

"Ha! I's no tell you's!"

"I say we kill him now and get it over with," Hydrib muttered, arms crossed about his chest.

"Fine! I's not scared of you's!" The orc puffed out his chest and frowned, somehow managing to make his face even uglier. Without a word Hydrib unsheathed one of his numerous swords.

"Wait," Seramin said stopping Hydrib as he prepared to drive his blade through the creature's throat, "maybe we could use him."

"Use him?"

"Use I's?"

"As a guide. Living here in the mountains by himself this orc must know the fastest way to the fortresses."

"How about it, orc, will you be our guide?"

"No! I's don't serve humans!"

"Would you trade it for your life?" Seramin placed the tip of a dagger against the orc's throat, pressing down hard enough to draw a drop of blood. A flicker of fear crossed the creature's eyes.

"Maybe I's can."

* * * * *

With hands bound behind his back the orc plodded through the mountains, showing the captors the way to the nearest fort. "It be's four days from here's," he said with a mighty frown. Four days of being a prisoner to these humans did not appeal to the orc. And, once they reached the fort, death would probably be waiting in the form of an executioner's block. Humans didn't show kindness to orcs; they were hated and despised by everyone.

Shoshe was once again carried by Seramin—Hydrib had refused—and she remained silent, quietly mourning her losses. The captain could not think of a way to make her feel better so he talked to the orc; Hybrid had refused to speak to him earlier.

"So, orc, what is your home like?"

"It is nice, better than yours'es castles. We's lives in caves, build we's homes da."

"So, you found a cave to live in these mountains?"

"No." The orc shook its mighty green head. "No good caves here. Too small."

"Too small? How big are the caves in the orcish lands?"

"Big!" The orc would have spread his arms out wide if they hadn't been tied behind its back. "Thousands of orcs live da."

"Then where do you live?" Seramin questioned. He had never spoken to an orc before, and his curiosity about the beast continued to grow.

"I's build house," the orc stated proudly, "between's two trees, with a roof." He beamed at Seramin while telling about his house. In reality, it was a shack, but that was the style of orcish buildings, just pieces of scrap wood that had been nailed together and lashed down with rope, vines, and sometimes even chains. Whatever they could get their hands on.

The first night after capturing the orc they did not stop and make camp, but kept moving through the mountains because Hydrib reported seeing several groups of Northerners following their trail through the snow. They were perhaps a mile away, but Seramin didn't want to give them a chance to catch up and pushed the group throughout the night. Orcs have excellent night vision and their captive easily guided them onwards; being captured by the Northerners did not appeal to the orc either. Seramin made sure the orc remained faithful with its directions by keeping a sword pointed at his back.

On the second night they were all ready to collapse and Seramin regretfully called a halt. The orc was tied to a nearby tree; pine branches spread on the ground as makeshift beds. No fire was built; the captain wanted to give their pursuers no help in finding them. The night became very cold and sleep became near impossible. Shoshe complained about the cold so Seramin gave her half of his furs and she finally fell into a restless sleep. He sat up straight, shivering and listening to the never-ending howl of the wind.

The orc, making the best of its position, used the snow as a wind breaker and burrowed deep into the white powder until only his head was visible. He shivered uncontrollably, but at least the orc could survive the night. A wolf howled in the distance; another answered from across the mountain. Seramin closed his eyes and listen to the two animals as they talked to each other.

"Beautiful, is it not?" Hydrib asked from his bed between two pitiful evergreen saplings.

"Yes," Seramin agreed, noting that this was the first time that the prisoner had called anything beautiful.

"At first glance a wolf looks docile and kind, harmless to a person that knows better. But if threatened, or angry, the wolf's mask disappears and you discover the true being that lives in the grey fur. It could rip your throat open in seconds; crush bone in its powerful jaws. You cannot see true beauty until you can see animal that can kill its prey that is three times its own size."

"How do you not know that a wolf's anger is not the true mask, and that it is a very friendly animal?"

"All animals are evil, humans the most. We kill for no reason at all; at least a wolf only bites when hungry, or when attacked. We kill for reasons such as anger, or lust, or revenge. Humans kill thousands in a single day while an animal will kill one or two beings at the most."

"You cannot think that all humans are evil. There are some of us that are good inside."

"If you truly believe that, then you must agree that not all of the Northerners are evil," Hydrib's eyes flashed in the darkness, "and that some fight for a good and just cause."

"There may be a few."

Another howl cut through the air, this one much closer than the others.

"What do you think they're saying?"

Hydrib shrugged his shoulders, climbed to his feet, and walked off into the darkness, no longer willing to talk. Seramin eventually slipped into sleep, but his sleep was restless, his dreams filled with monsters and daemons that chased him about the mountain.

* * * * *

"A true's warrior shows his's trophies," the orc explained as the band climbed yet another mountain on their difficult journey.

"You's is not a great warrior until you's got trophies. Trophies means honor."

"What would an orc know about honor?" Seramin snapped. "All that you do is plunder and kill."

"We's only do's that because you's humans do the same's to us. If we's no steal, then we's starve."

"You kill entire towns!"

"You's do the same," the orc said in a dull whisper.

A restless and cold night had put the entire group on edge. Frostbite clung to the sides of their faces, noses running with mucous. Shoshe had been plagued with a hacking cough that shook her frail body with each spasm. If Hydrib suffered he did not show it. Plowing through the deep snow the man only scowled; steam rising from his body from the effort.

The barbarians had not stopped to make camp as Seramin had hoped and had closed the gap between the two groups during the night. From the heights of a tall ridge the captain watched as dozens of black shapes trudged along, following the unmistakable trail that they had created in the snow. Hounds bayed, pulling desperately on their tethers as they searched out the scent of their prey.

"Orcs is a proud race," the green-skin continued once again, "honor's everything's in battle. Prove's my's self I's hat."

"Is it true, that the orcs came from the underworld?" Shoshe asked in a tiny voice. The other three stopped and turned to stare at the girl in amazement. This was the most that she had spoken in over a day.

"Yes, that be true." The orc held his head in shame. "But we's better now."

"I doubt it," Seramin retorted. "I spent over two years in the east fighting your kind. You didn't take prisoners, you butchered them."

"Surrender's dishonor. It's is very bad."

Hydrib gave the orc a sideways glance. "Strange how you are our prisoner at the moment."

"I's not like's the other orcs. I's different."

"Is that why you were exiled, because you were different?"

The orc refused to answer. Turning its ugly face away the creature continued to move at his slow pace.

For three days the orc led the humans closer to the fortress. Each day the Northerners continued to close in, forcing the band to run without rest. All except Hydrib developed colds and began to cough uncontrollably. Shoshe became sick with a fever, her forehead burning as if on fire. Cuddled in Seramin's arms the girl called out to her dead father. Sometimes she would scream and claw at her face. It broke his heart to know that he could do nothing to ease her pain.

A thin stream of smoke appeared in the distance; curling into the air from a distant bluff. Greot pointed to the oily smudge with a fat finger and gave a grave look. "That there's the fortress."

The atmosphere became even more solemn after that. Could it be that the Northerners had pushed this far? Had the fortress been sacked? If so, how many Northerners would be in hiding when they arrived? There seemed no other choice but to push ahead and continue towards the trail of smoke. The band was running low on supplies, and there was no town for many miles in any direction. Hydrib suggested killing the orc to save on food, but Seramin would not allow that. He was not inclined to kill in cold blood if he could help it. He was not an animal. He was not an orc.

During the night the bluff would light up with explosions and an orange glow as fires erupted. Through the cold mountain air the long, stretched-out wails of the dying and the heavy grunts and clashes of battle could be heard. The fighting continued deep into the night. The situation for the defenders seemed grim, but the fighting gave the band hope, for there the fortress still held.

The path became more and more difficult, forcing them to scale sheer cliffs and to wade through neck-high snowdrifts. Hydrib grunted and groaned with effort, struggling to move while carrying his cumbersome sword. Seramin suggested leaving it, since it served no purpose but to hold them back. Hydrib retorted by suggesting to leave Shoshe behind, for the only purpose she served was to hold the group back.

Chapter 8
The Fortress

The fourth night of the journey to the fortress proved to be the coldest by far. A harsh wind blew through the trees, ripping the warmth from skin with the savageness of a wolf. Trees exploded as the water in their veins expanded to the breaking point, bursting the trunk as if a bomb. Shoshe sobbed as frostbite grabbed at her tender skin, Greot's tusked teeth chattered violently, and Seramin did his best not to cry.

"Tears would probably freeze to my face," he mumbled.

Hydrib seemed to be the least affected. He refused to cover his face, looking straight into the wind as if daring Mother Nature to do her worst. She screamed in fury at his resilience, but he only roared back at her with a silent voice.

Unable to move another step Seramin fell to his knees, dropping Shoshe in a snow bank. The orc followed suit; Hydrib glared at them for their weakness, but then sat down himself. Forming a circle the three conscious members of the band looked into each other's faces, trying to read their thoughts. Three miserable enemies near the brink of death. Each unwilling to accept a friendship with the other.

"Now what?" Hydrib growled.

"We wait here until daylight. Then, we continue moving to the fortress. It can't be far."

"What of the Northerners then?"

"I doubt they will continue their search in this weather."

"Do not doubt the North's resolve."

"Even if they haven't made camp tonight there's no chance of finding us. The wind has blown away our trail, it's too dark to see, and the wind is blowing the wrong way. Those hounds will never pick up our scent."

"What's about us? I's cold."

"This is nothing compared to some of the nights by the Yatzi River," Seramin stuttered. "It was so cold at night that our swords were snapping in half."

"I doubt that."

"No, I swear that it's true. We would strike our weapons against a tree and the metal would break."

"That cold," the orc marveled.

"Yep. A-and some of the men would wake up in the morning with their mouths frozen shut!"

Over the sound of the wailing wind footsteps stomped and weapons smashed against shields. Sitting still, remaining deathly silent, the trio listened to the sounds of an army as it marched past. Obscure shapes drifted in and out of the trees, limbs of trees snapped as men marched past. Grunts and groans carried through the wind as the warriors struggled against the bitter elements. Some carried torches, leading sweating teams as they strained against ropes, dragging siege weapons over the rough terrain.

Seramin's blood turned cold as he watched hundreds, thousands of shadows move through the woods, oblivious of the group as it huddled in the open. His eyes spied Shoshe, still lying unconscious in the snow. If she woke up in one of her feverish rants, screaming and crying… it would be all over. But, for the moment, she remained still. Lying low in the snow Seramin risked a glance towards Hydrib; his mouth fell open when noticing that the prisoner had disappeared. The orc was gone as well. Had they run off, or were they simply in hiding?

Some of the warriors came close enough to Seramin for him to see their faces. Their bodies brushed against pine branches, knocking their loads of powdery snow onto the captain's prone body. He dared not flinch. Without so much as a second look the barbarians continued their journey. Loud commands echoed through the night, cutting the silence like a knife before being carried away in the wind.

A man emerged, squeezing his bulky body between a pair of buckthorn bushes; cracking of twigs loud and augmented. Seramin flinched at the noise. Then, his breath caught in his throat as the man took a step forwards, moving towards the body of Shoshe. As if in slow motion the warrior moved closer until his boot nearly touched the girl's leg. Then, ever so slowly, he stepped over the obstacle without contact. Seramin granted himself a brief sigh of relief. If the warrior had happened to stumble upon the girl the alarm would have been sounded. Even with the aid of the prisoner Seramin knew that he was no match for a hundred battle-seasoned Northerners.

Moving stealthily from behind a tree Hydrib appeared, a knife in his hand. Taking careful steps he began to sneak up on the warrior. Seramin tried to get the prisoner's attention, shaking his head without allowing the Northerner to see him. Ignoring the captain's pleas Hydrib moved closer, preparing to deliver a killing blow. That was when a twig snapped beneath his foot. Everyone froze, holding their breaths, ears searching for the slightest hint of noise.

Seramin's stomach twisted into a knot. All it would take was one shout, one cry for help and it would be all over.

The Northerner jerked backwards as something struck his chest, his body twitching as death set upon his body. Hydrib ducked back at the sudden attack. Falling to his knees the barbarian gave a final gurgle, and then fell limply to the ground. A stream of hot steam poured from the open wound.

The air became alive with the buzzing of an angry swarm of bees. Arrows filled the forest, slamming into tree trucks with loud thunks or sifting beneath the snow with low phtts. Shadows fell beneath the barrage. Screaming in fear they took shelter behind whatever was available.

A loud crash sounded as the night sky lit up with a flash of blue. Men screamed in pain and fright as the spell ripped through their ranks. Flaming arrows crisscrossed through the air, leaving trails of burning wool like miniature kite tails. Smoke, ugly choking columns, billowed into the air. The Northern sorcerers began casting their own spells, but before they could complete them tongues of flame jumped from the darkness; trees burst into flames, men's flesh melted from their bones.

"Get down!" Another bolt of lightning ripped through the trees; several split in half, creating a domino effect as each fell.

Hydrib grunted, a sliver of wood embedded in his shoulder. Without hesitating he ripped the bloody shrapnel from his flesh. Blood spurted out in tiny bursts, dribbling down the front of his shirt. Knocking aside the maze of branches that now covered the ground he began to push towards a cluster of thorny bushes. A hard kick caused the bush to yelp in pain. Poking his head out the orc frowned.

"Do not dare hide while others fight!" the prisoner roared, grabbing the orc by the neck, and throwing the creature out into the open with ease. Spitting snow from his mouth the orc snarled.

"I's no die for human!"

"Neither will I."

The band had managed to creep within fifty yards of the fortress without realizing it. Now they where caught in the middle of the siege. Arrows criss-crossed the air in all directions. Spells danced in the night sky, destroying regiments of warriors, killing by the handfuls. Now firepots began to fall as well.

Tumbling end over end a heavy ceramic pot with a flaming rag attached to one end struck a tree, bouncing from limb to limb until the pot broke, spilling pitch onto the ground which ignited in a rush of red-hot flame. The forest lit up with the explosion. Dozens of Northerners milled about, flames licking at their clothes. Many of their screams became snuffed out as the fire worked its way into their lungs.

With the burst of light and heat from the firepot Shoshe awoke. Screams of rage and pain found their way into her ears. The air seemed alive with the battle between the overpowering heat of the fires and the bitter cold of the winter. Delirious from the fever she began to scream. One long endless wail.

"Silence!" Seramin shouted. Crawling on hands and knees he threw himself upon the thrashing girl, a hand smothering her cries.

"Let me go! Let me go!"

"Calm down, everything will be fine!"

The words felt like poison in his mouth. Arrows fell around them. The bodies of barbarians, many of them wounded, lay around them. Those not killed or injured raced towards the fortress, jumping over the captain as he struggled to control the girl. The battle so chaotic they could not even notice the two. Slowly, Shoshe began to calm. She fell limp in the captain's arms, her screams turning to those of sobs. "Cold, I'm so cold."

"Just wait a moment," Seramin pleaded.

"No," the girl gave a violent shake of her head, "stop the cold. Please."

"Alright."

Hooking his arms under the small body Seramin lifted Shoshe, clutching her to his chest. Then, with a grim look of determination on his face, his legs churning for all they were worth, the captain ran towards the fortress. Northerners fell and died all about him. He jumped over the wounded. Arrows hissed like snakes, their invisible paths determined by fate. Branches slashed at Seramin's face, ripping his raw skin open. Discarded weapons, shields, equipment, and dead bodies snagged his legs and threatened to trip him.

Finally, he reached his destination; a ring of fire created from a firepot. A pile of pine trees had ignited from the weapon and now the wood crackled and hissed. The heat struck Seramin like a wall as he set Shoshe down into the melting snow. A loud thud next to him marked the arrival of the orc, soon followed by Hydrib.

Throughout all the chaos Seramin was glad to be warm. All through the night they huddled together, wishing for the killing to stop; all except Hydrib. He grinned and watched the killing with glee.

Chapter 9
Aagon

Birds sang. How could birds sing after what had occurred that night? The Northerners threw wave after wave against the mighty fortress throughout the entire night. Once the sun began to break across the landscape the army retreated, preventing the defenders from finding targets to aim their arrows.

After the sound of battle had left the mountainside the sounds of the wounded began. Men screamed, dying in the snow. Some cried out names, others curses against their enemies. The screams dwindled as time wore on, loss of blood and the cold taking their victims.

Crawling into the open Seramin scanned the battlefield. Bodies littered the ground creating a carpet of corpses. Small fires continued to burn, eating away at the charred remains of once proud and mighty trees. Hidden behind a thin veil of smoke was the fortress wall.

Small in relative terms, the walls only reached a meager ten feet tall and the door consisted of rough pine logs nailed together. The remains of a battering ram lay broken by the door, which was dented and cracked. Ladders still leaned against the walls, dead bodies lodged between the steps. They swung side to side with the wind. Long, bloody stains trailed down the wall's stone ledge. Dead could be seen lying on the battlements.

"What do you think?" the captain asked turning to see the prisoner's expression.

"I think your idea is crazy."

"Well, it's either get into the fortress or wait for the Northerners to return tonight."

"Yes, but walking up to the wall? The garrison will shoot you on sight. They won't even bother with hearing your pleas."

"What do you suggest then, storming the walls?"

"At least we would have a chance then."

Seramin held his arms out wide in an expression of peace. As he moved closer to the wall the blurred shapes of guards could be seen, scourging the battle grounds for any sign of enemy intruders. Seramin's heart pounded like a hammer in his chest, but he did not dare turn back. Survival depended on entering the fortress. Coming within thirty feet of the walls he stopped and tilted his head back, shouting a greeting.

"Defenders of this fortress, I am Captain Seramin of the Southern army. I call for you to allow me and my companions to enter."

A moment of silence passed before an answer drifted through the smoke.

"What would a fellow soldier be doing outside of the walls? We have only seen the enemy as of late."

"I was on my way to the front; I was then attacked by the Northern barbarians and followed here."

"Why should we believe you?" the voice scrutinized.

"Is my presence in the open not proof enough?"

Garbled voices reached Seramin's ears as several of the guards debated. A few shouts came through the conversation, but they were quickly hushed.

"Who are these companions that you speak of?"

Seramin licked his lips nervously and began thinking of an answer. He needed to pick his words carefully, for it was doubtful that the defenders of the fortress would be willing to allow an orc and a man such as Hydrib into their haven. All men despised orcs, and had spent countless centuries trying to eradicate the monsters. Hydrib had the appearance of a barbarian due to his ragged clothes and wide assortment of weaponry. It would be easy for a guard to mistake him as an enemy at first glance.

"There are three others with me. A fellow soldier, a small girl, and a native of the mountains."

Anther round of discussion ensued before the guard spoke again. "You will be allowed to enter. Bring your band to the gate, but be warned. If any aggression is taken against us you will be killed."

With much effort the defenders pried open the badly damaged doors just enough so that Seramin and the others could squeeze through. Once they had passed through the portal the soldiers slammed the doors shut and began nailing boards back into place. While holding a sickly Shoshe in his arms Seramin was greeted by a man dressed in a flowing grey robe. A vanguard of ten soldiers stood by the man's side, cautiously eying the newcomers.

"Greetings, my son," the priest said with a grandfatherly smile. The grin split the large beard that covered his face; two rows of white teeth shining from within black. Locks of black hair with streaks of grey flowed down onto the man's neck. Two tree-trunk arms rested easily at his side; as the priest moved Seramin noted the muscles that rippled and bulged through the fabric.

"Greetings, Father." Seramin returned the welcome with a nod of his head.

"My brothers will take care of the child," the priest said motioning to Shoshe. "They are very skilled in the healing arts. She will be safe with them."

Two small men dressed in identical grey robes as the priest appeared at Seramin's side. He reluctantly handed over the girl, who was whisked away by the lesser priests. With his release on Shoshe Seramin's exhaustion washed over him like a wave. His legs weakening the captain tipped over to the side, leaning heavily against the wall.

"It appears that you have had a most difficult journey," the priest noted glancing from Seramin's tired face to Hydrib's despicable style of dress.

The captain nodded his head wearily. "The Northerners destroyed a small village by the name of Talron four or five days ago; that is the girl's home. We have been running ever since."

A chorus of angry shouts sounded as the orc's true identity was revealed, his hood thrown off of his mangy head. The sound of metal on metal sounded as dozens of swords, spears, and halberds where drawn and pointed at the green-skin. He snarled, but remained still. "I's already tied up. How's I's hurt you's?" He glared at the ring of humans around him.

The priest's face revealed his puzzlement as he looked at the creature, studying it. "And for what reason is an orc a member of your companionship?"

"Long story," Hydrib remarked. Seramin quickly took over.

"We found him living in the mountains a few days out, he acted as our guide to the fortress."

"You managed to tame an orc? Interesting." The captain forgotten, the priest walked up to the orc, pushing aside weapons so that he could get a closer look. "I have seen many orcs in my day, but never one so calm as this... by the will of the gods."

"Fightin' just get I's killed faster."

"And an intelligent orc as well. My, my, what an interesting specimen it is."

The priest turned his back to the orc. "I's have's a name you's know."

He paused. "What did you say?"

"I's said I's have's a name. I's be Greot."

"Greot? Well I happen to be Aagon, high warrior priest of Jipniv."

"Fancy title," the prisoner laughed, "not that I'm at all impressed."

"I'm sorry, I almost forgot you there. I don't believe Seramin told me your name."

"He didn't."

"Mind telling me what it is then?"

"In fact I do mind." Hydrib straightened to his full height, making the powerful priest appear tiny in his shadow.

"His name is Hydrib," Seramin intervened softly.

"Hydrib?" Aagon's face scrunched up as if trying to remember something. "Interesting name... Hydrib." Shaking his head the priest caught sight of the collar that clung to the prisoner's neck. He eyed the strange object before shrugging it off and returning to Seramin.

"I presume that you and your...friend, Hydrib, will need a meal and a change of clothes. Unfortunately, because of the siege supplies are beginning to run low, but I'm sure the cooks will find something suitable for you."

"Yes, thank you." Seramin's eyes trailed over to Greot.

"Oh, yes, as for the orc I believe that it is best if he is chained up. We don't want anything *else* going wrong."

A number of soldiers proceeded to push at Greot, forcing the orc away from the gate. Giving a howl of rage the orc fought against the humans, but the overwhelming numbers soon overcame his hunger-weakened frame. As he disappeared around a corner the priest gave a small bow. "Please, let me guide you to the kitchen." A big smile crossed his face. "The gods of good are always willing to serve those of the same faith."

Leading the pair of newcomers to the kitchen Aagon pointed out the damage that the attackers had caused to the fortress, and explained the situation. "We have been under siege for the last five days or so. We kill hundreds of the unholy scum with each attack that they throw at us, but it seems that their numbers are inexhaustible. Now we are nearly out of food, and running out of men. The best officer that we can muster is a sergeant, which means that you are the senior ranking officer, and leader of this fortress, Seramin, after me of course."

"Of course."

Buildings lay in ruin, the result of a constant bombardment from heavy catapults. Walls collapsed, creating mounds of rubble that required to be navigated. Fires had ravaged the fortress, scorching the walls black and gutting out warehouses. Mounds of bodies sat in the corners, stacked like cork board. With the ground frozen it was impossible for the defenders to bury their dead. Once killed a body was taken to the drop-off and stored away to be taken care of later.

Soldiers stopped in their work to stare at the trio as they walked past. What had these men brought with them? They thought as they sized up Seramin and the prisoner. A faint glimmer of hope jumped to their hearts before being dashed. Two men would not turn the tide of this battle.

The cook managed to scrounge up two bowls of watery soup and some cheese and bread which Seramin attacked viciously. After gulping down the soup he felt guilty about asking for seconds, but the bowl was refilled before he could say a word. Hydrib chomped noisily at his bread, jaw popping with each bite. Aagon grimaced at the sound. The prisoner did not seem to notice and continued to rip into the bread. Pop. Pop. Pop.

"Once you two are finished eating I will show you to the armory. Considering that you are now here it would be best to be properly armed, and dressed," the priest added quickly when Hydrib shot him a look.

"I appreciate that, but I wish to see the girl as soon as possible."

"Of course," Aagon spread his calloused hands out over the table. "She will be in the field hospital."

After finishing the meal, a growling belly finally quieted, Seramin pushed away the dishes in front of him and requested that the priest lead the way to the hospital. Once entering the only building that seemed to be mostly intact the wave of smells hit Seramin, washing over his body and bringing him back to the horrors of the battlefield. Countless wounded lay on the floor in neat rows so that the few overworked healers could move more efficiently. Blood covered the floor. Hidden behind walls of sheets doctors worked to saw off the bloody stumps of mangled limbs. The patients screeched horribly as the savage work continued. Pale-faced men walked past carrying buckets loaded with hands, arms, and even whole legs.

Aagon moved through a door leading to a separate room. Inside a pair of tables surrounded by a horde of chairs took up all available space. Shoshe sat on one of the tables, a healer working to remove the bloody bandages. "We thought it best to keep the girl away from the others..." Aagon motioned towards the location of the screams and moans of pain.

"Is someone there?" Shoshe questioned timidly from her perch.

"Yes," Aagon cooed as if talking to a newborn, "two of the men that brought you here have come to visit."

Shoshe made as if to reply, but then slumped over, shaking violently. The healer pulled her upright.

"She's suffering from a terrible fever. I gave her a dose of healing magic, but the infection is coming from the wound on her face. I need to clean it or else the infection will continue to grow worse."

With the utmost care the man peeled away the final layers of cloth. It took all of Seramin's strength not to gasp. A mat of dried gore and oozing blood covered Shoshe's once-beautiful face. Two black pits from where her eyes should have been glared out from the bloody mess. Cuts covered the area that surrounded her now-destroyed eyes. A film of yellowish-green growth sprouted from the mangled mass of flesh.

"Gods protect her," Aagon muttered as he crossed himself.

"Am I still pretty?" the girl asked, the fever throwing off her thoughts.

"The prettiest girl I've ever seen," the healer whispered, tears in his eyes as he told the lie. "Now just stay here and I'll be back in a moment."

He left Shoshe and moved towards Seramin and Aagon; Hydrib had moved away and leaned against the wall in the corner, arms crossed and head looking down at the ground. "Well?" Seramin hissed none too gently.

"The wound is infected. It needs to be cleaned. I have a potion that will work, but I need someone to hold her down."

"I will do it," the priest said without hesitation, moving to the girl's side.

"No," a hand touched his shoulder, "I'll do it." Seramin's face grim.

"Are you sure?"

"Yes."

"Just make sure you don't let go of her, no matter how much she screams or fights. If the potion doesn't soak in then we'll have to do it all over again," the healer warned. Seramin nodded his head in understanding.

Shoshe swayed from side to side as her weak body struggled to sit upright at the table. Her destroyed face looking around in a sightless stare.

"Sweetie, I need you to lie down."

"Why?" The healer had to avert his eyes as the face swiveled to look at him.

"I just need to do one more thing."

He gently pushed Shoshe back until she rested flat on the table. Seramin gripped her head between his hands. The healer then took a vial from his pocket and pulled out the cork stopper.

"What's going on?" Shoshe whimpered as she felt the strong hands of Seramin closing about her head. Unable to give the girl an answer Seramin merely nodded for the healer to continue. Once the liquid hit her open wounds Shoshe gave a bloodcurdling scream. Her fists punched out into the air. Dropping the vial the healer threw himself on the girl to hold her body down.

Smoke billowed from Shoshe's face as the potion burned away the infection. Two columns of steam shot out from her eyes giving the girl a daemonic look. Seramin struggled to hold her head in place, the pain giving Shoshe a great spurt of strength. Aagon jumped to their aid in order to keep the girl down. As the potion finished its task the burning began to cease. Shoshe's movements slowed, and then she eventually became limp.

* * * * *

"Is all prepared?" Pouja whispered to the priest.

"Nearly… a few more minutes are required before the ritual can take place."

"Well, hurry then, Sinji waits for no man."

The priest gave a bow before hurrying away. It was not wise to anger the king.

Now late into the night Pouja and a number of priests circled around the altar in his quarters. Chained to the stone slab of the altar a young girl of seventeen years stared wide-eyed at the barbarians that circled around her. She was a native Southerner that had been captured by the invading forces, and that was being given the greatest honor of Sinji's followers. But this she did not know.

Chanting ancient incantations the priests poured human blood on her body, forming ancient runes with the liquid. Too terrified to speak, the girl could only look up at them with wide eyes. The cold liquid burned deep into her bones. Unable to help herself the girl began to shiver. Flecks of blood splashed onto her lips and she tried to spit them away.

The last object to be placed in the ritual was a magnificent golden crown. Shimmering in the candlelight the crown seemed to dance in the high priest's hands as he brought it forwards. Slowly, carefully, he placed it on the girl's head. She looked around, confused about what was going on. What was the crown for?

Watching impassionedly Pouja paced the floor. His hand rubbed the stubble on his chin. Gone was the mass of black armor, replaced with a dark robe, complete with a flowing cape with a trim of gold fabric. A ceremonial sword in a silver-finished scabbard bounced absentmindedly against his hip. Well-worn riding boots clicked against the polished floorboards.

"All is ready," the head dark priest notified quietly. A nervous hand pushed away a strand of greasy, brown hair from his watery brown eyes. The man trembled slightly as the massive form of the king appeared before him in two gigantic steps. Cowering away from his leader the man glanced at the sword. Not that the king would need it if he wished to dispose of the worthless whelp. The big hands could snap the priest's neck with one powerful twist.

"Proceed then."

"Yes, my lord, but it will take several minutes. The incantations are strange to us—"

"I don't care for your excuses. This ritual was passed down by the goddess herself. It is correct... and it will work." Pouja leaned over so that he looked the priest in the eyes. "Get on with it." His hiss released the scent of rotten meat and old vegetables.

"Y-yes, my lord."

"And don't let me catch you questioning me again."

The other priests watched as their superior shrank before Pouja without any remorse in their hearts. Better him than us, they thought. The high priest would set his anger and fear on the lesser members of the dark order, but they did not fear him as they did the king.

Forming a ring around the altar the priests began to chant the incantations that they had struggled to memorize that morning. Moving faster and faster through the chant the priests' voices grew into a dull roar as the power of the spell began to flow through their bodies. Their hair began to stand on end, electricity tingled against their skin. Ecstasy like nothing the priests had felt began to surge through their veins.

Pouja's face broke into a grin as the events began to unfold. Years of fighting for power, years of following the goddess's orders to the letter, now his hard labors would take fruit. Looking down at the girl on the altar his smile grew even wider. "The goddess thanks you for your service."

A strong wind began to blow inside the room, forcing the priests to scream over the roar. Sweat dripped from their red faces. Some shook from the effort of keeping the spell in check. Pouja's robes whipped violently against his side. Despite the vortex of wind the candles that illuminated his chambers did not so much as flicker.

The girl tensed with fear as she felt the power of the spell touching her skin, sending quick bursts of energy into her body. Then, suddenly, the chanting ceased and the wind came to a halt. The robes of the priests fluttered back to the ground. All was calm.

Then a jolt of pain shot through the girl's body. Screaming she yanked at the chains that held her, but they refused to budge. More pain continued to shoot through her as she wracked her body, writhing like a landed fish.

Pouja watched the girl squirm.

The girl's hair color began to change. Starting at the roots the golden curls slowly transformed into straight black hair that grew until it reached the girl's waist. Her facial features began to morph and move like hot wax, changing appearance until she had the look of a young adult of twenty-five. When her eyes changed from blue to yellow her screams turned to wild hisses of a snake.

* * * * *

Bundled against the cold Seramin stood on the ramparts overlooking the cliff face. Seeing no sign of the Northerners worried him. He had no idea if the barbarians would attack tonight, or if the defeat had hurt them badly enough to force a permanent retreat. With the fall of darkness the wall guard tripled. Every ten feet a soldier armed with a halberd stood at attention, eyes searching for the slightest sign of danger.

Seramin stood for several more minutes, waiting for the sun to set behind the mountains; watching as his breath turned to frost. As the air turned grey with the coming of night the captain turned and descended the stairs into the courtyard. A pair of guards gave a quick salute as the superior officer passed by. So deep in his thoughts Seramin almost forgot to return the sign.

No light shined inside the confines of the wall. Aagon had explained that the barbarians used light to aim their catapults during the night. The siege weapons had proved too weak to break through the thick stone walls, but the defenders' lives became a living hell as they suffered through bombardments that lasted throughout the night. Coming to the dark outline of a building, its left wall sporting man-sized holes from catapults, Seramin knocked twice on the door. A yellow crack appeared as a guard inside came to see who was there.

"Captain Seramin to see priest Aagon."

"Enter."

Stomping the snow from his boots Seramin hurried over to a wood stove that crackled merrily. Three more guards huddled over the small source of heat; rubbing their hands furiously. Another guard sat at a badly splintered table, trying to break up the ice in his cup. The holes had been covered with black cloth in order to keep in the light more than to keep out the cold. Cold wormed through the cloth, turning the room into an ice box.

"It's quiet out there," Seramin stated, referring to the absence of the barbarians.

"Ay," a guard with a bloody bandage around his head said, "that's the way those bloody bastards work. They stay out of sight so we can never know if they're simply sleeping or if they're trying to sneak up on us. It drives the wall guards crazy, keeps them out there all night searchin' for bloody ghosts."

A high-pitched whistle sounded, followed by a loud boom and a wave of crackling sounds as if someone had thrown ice cubes onto a slab of ice. Seramin jumped at the sound, but none of the guards moved.

"Hit the wall," a soldier wrapped tightly in a blanket muttered.

"After a while you can tell where the catapult rounds land just by the noise," the first guard explained. "It's become a sort of game for us."

"Some game."

The guard shrugged. "We need to find a way to pass the time somehow." Another whistle sounded, this one followed by a dull thud. "Hit the ground, probably in the courtyard somewhere."

The third whistle grew louder than the others, ringing in Seramin's ears. "This one is gonna be close," the guard at the table said.

With a mighty crash the circular rock burst through the wall, traveling through the room tossing furniture aside as it went before crashing through the other side of the building. Dust filled the room, creating a choking cloud of powdered mortar and brick. "Yep, pretty close," the guard said as he resumed picking at the ice.

"Gods damn it!" the guard with the blanket cursed. Grabbing a handful of snow he threw it into the stove to snuff out the fire. "Can't keep the fire going or the catapults will keep shooting at us," he explained to Seramin.

Getting to his feet Seramin brushed off the fine layer of white powder from his jacket. Sneezing and coughing his body fought to get the dust from his lungs.

"Might as well go up and see Aagon," a voice said in the dying light of the embers; Seramin could not tell which guard said this. "It will be warmer in his chambers than in here." Giving a final cough as a reply Seramin found the stairs in the dark and then moved to the second floor. A thin crack of yellow on the floor led the captain to Aagon's chamber door. A heavy voice bellowed from behind the door after Seramin knocked.

"Come in, come in! No need for formalities."

"Sorry, Father, I did not want to interrupt you."

"You are not interrupting, my son; after all, I was the one that sent for you. Have a seat, relax." The priest's hand pointed to and empty seat.

Bookshelves crammed with volumes upon volumes of leather-bound books and stacks of parchment lined the walls. Paper bulged from every corner. The musty smell of a library could be detected in the cold room. A desk took up a good portion of the room's space. Even more books sat on the desk; many stacked in towering piles. A chalice half filled with wine rested on the edge of the desk. Made of copper the chalice shone in the flickering candlelight. Near a small, cloth-covered window, a tiny shrine dedicated to the sun gods overlooked the room.

Picking up the chalice Aagon took a sip of the red liquid. "I would offer you some wine, Captain, but it took me the better part of an hour to thaw out what you see here."

"That is fine, I don't drink."

"Oh? A shame then." Taking another swig of the wine the priest set the chalice down. "The healers report that the girl's fever is falling, it seems that the potion is doing the trick."

"That is a relief to hear."

"She your daughter?"

"What, daughter? No," Seramin stuttered, thrown back by the question, "no, she comes from Talron. I was there when the Northerners attacked. Her father died in the raid."

"Oh, I'm sorry to hear that. But, he is now in a better place."

"Yes, let us hope so."

Aagon shook his head sending locks of hair flying into his face. Sitting down in his seat behind the desk he gave out a loud sigh. "A strange sight your band made coming in here. You, a soldier, the girl, an orc, and that man… What was his name?"

"Hydrib," Seramin answered quickly wanting to avoid the subject of the prisoner.

"Ah, yes, Hydrib. Is that man from Talron too?"

"No, but that is where I met him." Seramin was technically not lying.

"Have you noticed the collar on the man's neck? I'm sure you have, but I am curious abut it. There is something about that collar that is … amiss."

Seramin subconsciously scratched at his own collar hidden beneath the folds of his robe. His skin began to sweat despite the winter weather. He did not want to find out how the priest would act once learning of the prisoner's true, most likely unholy origins. "There are many things about that man that are strange."

"Yes, especially that sword of his. I've never seen anything like it before. I tried deciphering the runes on the blade but I did not understand them, even though I am versed in several tongues."

"What about the orc?" Seramin asked hoping to change the subject.

"Yes, the orc." Aagon settled back in his chair and gave a laugh. "That creature is chained outside at a pole, but don't worry," he said quickly seeing Seramin's concern for the green-skin, "the orc has been supplied with enough furs to keep it warm throughout the night."

Seramin nodded his head. "I thank you for that. If it was not for Greot we would not have survived in the mountains. I daresay I owe my life to that orc. It was he that showed us the way to the fortress."

Aagon's smile faded and his face turned grim. Looking down at his hands he shifted uncomfortably. "I am afraid that you have only prolonged your fate. The Northerners have weakened the forces here, breaking the men's spirits. Already I am down to three hundred from a force that once measured nearly seven hundred strong. I believe that the barbarians are building their forces, and are preparing to send a final attack against our walls."

"Is there not any chance of holding out?"

"Only the gods know the answer to questions like that." The priest gave a wounded smile.

Seramin's heart fell. He had led himself from one bad situation to another; this one seemingly worse. The only bright side was that he had at least brought the prisoner into battle. Unfortunately, the girl was once again in the face of danger. The captain vowed to fight to the last. The girl would not be harmed again while he lived.

"You have my sword, Father Aagon."

"Thank you, Captain. Me and the men will need all the help that we can get come tomorrow."

Chapter 10
The Goddess of Blood

Watching herself in the mirror Sinji flicked her mane of glistening black hair over her shoulders and smiled. It had been a long time since she had walked in the Realm of the Living and had almost forgotten how good it felt not to be breathing in toxic fumes, or to be broiled with the molten magma that crept up from the ground. The girl had been a good sacrifice, and her body suited Sinji perfectly, with a few modifications of course.

Although it required a great amount of strength it was possible for a god to take on a human form, but as a result Sinji left her kingdom in the Realm of the Dead in a weakened state, and her human form had only a fraction of the powers that she possessed in her true form. Still, but a small price to pay for what she sought in this realm.

Lifting a glass of wine to her lips the goddess tasted the sweet taste of the drink and smacked her red lips in delight. Oh, she had forgotten about the tastes of real food and drink! Her spidery fingers set the glass down; the crystal clinked silently upon the table.

A timid knock sounded at the door. "Yes?" Sinji called in a silky voice. The door opened slowly revealing a shaking man.

"Begging your pardon, your highness," the pitiful human messenger stammered in fear, "but King Pouja wishes to speak with you."

"Yes, please send in the king."

The man breathed a sigh of relief and hurried out of sight. Sinji watched his every move with her yellow eyes. Pouja shuffled into the room a few seconds later. Moving to the center of the room he fell to one knee in respect for his goddess.

"Rise," Sinji ordered; she never tired of the sight of a human groveling before her feet, but there were more important matters at hand. "What word of the weapon?"

"Sinji, I must report that my men cannot find the captain, or the weapon that he has in his possession. Twice my men fought the pair in battle, but they have managed to survive and elude our forces."

"What?" The goddess's voice rose to a shrill screech.

Pouja stumbled backwards as if struck a physical blow. "Please allow me to continue, mistress. My men have found the captain's trail and it will be only a moment before he is captured. The area is swarming with my men."

"I do not care for your excuses. I demand that the Southern captain and the prisoner be caught at once!" The walls shook as the outburst of rage released a burst of magic from Sinji's newly acquired human form. "It is wise that you do not fail me again, Pouja," she hissed angrily.

"Yes, goddess, forgive me."

Sinji calmed herself, and then moved to the king. Her long legs moved easily through the air, bare feet slapping softly against the floor. The golden crown that had once sat on the young girl's head now rested on the goddess's brow, glowing in the light of the hundreds of burning candles that filled the room. She laid a hand on her servant's shoulder.

"That is of little importance," she cooed into his ear as if forgetting her previous outburst. "We shall deal with this... nuisance later, but at the moment we have more important matters to attend to. I have heard that you are sending the main part of your forces to the east, as a diversion so that your men can capture the fortresses in the west."

"Yes, I thought that I could—"

"Do not speak!" the goddess roared. Pouja jumped a foot into the air. "I am not finished! Now, answer me, is this true?"

"Yes," Pouja whispered in fear. Lost in the venomous yellow eyes of the small woman in front of him the king felt a deep fear burning in his heart.

"Then you must turn the rest of your army back to the west."

"But why?"

"Because there is a more important prize in the mountains, something that will give you the greatest army that has ever walked upon this earth." Throwing her hands into the air Sinji accented her words with fluid motions of her spidery arms. "You will be unstoppable, and this mere... captain, will be only a gnat against you. But, whether they know it or not the Southerner and his prisoner are near the item. We must take it for ourselves before this item can be turned against us."

"What is in the mountains?" the king asked intently.

"The key to victory." Sinji smiled, licking her lips hungrily. "A magic item that has been lost upon this world since my imprisonment in the Realm of the Dead.

Chapter 11
Calm Before the Storm

Shaking snow from his body Greot peeked out from his burrow of furs. Frost crackled in the air with every breath, ice shattered from his diamond-encrusted hair with each shake of his head. Winter stung at his exposed flesh, biting down with tiny needles of pain. Accustomed to the harsh winters Greot shrugged off the mild discomfort and stretched to his full height of six feet four inches. Seeing the mass of green muscle rising from the ground the passing soldiers gave the orc a wide berth.

Greot smiled at the fear that the humans felt towards him. Even though chained to a post, unable to move, he instilled terror into the battle-toughened men. He snapped at one, exalted at the man's sudden jump to the side.

The hunched-over shape of Seramin caught Greot's eye as the captain stumbled out of a building, muscles stiff from sleeping on a stone floor. The human's eyes glazed over from lack of sleep, he snapped back at the sudden blast of arctic chill. Regaining his senses the man pulled the collar of his coat closer and began to push his way through the snow drifts.

"Good's morning's, human," Greot growled pleasantly. He tried to give a wave but the chains inhibited his movements to a two-fisted shake, metal rattling on the post.

"Hello, orc." Seramin smiled halfheartedly. "Sleep well?"

"I's was fine. My's cave warmer."

"I wouldn't doubt it."

Guards cried with glee as a volley of arrows cut down a group of Northerners that had wandered too close to the fortress. Several of the men had only been wounded and tried to crawl back to the safety of the woods but more and more arrows punched their way into their bodies until the life had flowed from them. Seramin and Greot turned their heads to watch the spectacle, the men laughing and shaking each other's arms as if watching an event in the arena.

"Northerners attack's soon." It was not a question.

"Yes."

"We's win?"

Seramin remained silent as he struggled for the right words, then gave up and just gave the orc the truth. "No, they are too many. We are too weak."

"Ah, I's wish to meet those men's with my's axe." Greot gave a sad look and motioned to his shackles. "I's fight for you's."

"No, we don't want your help." Seramin turned and walked away, continuing his journey to the hospital.

"You's need's me!"

* * * * *

"How are you feeling today, sweetie?" Aagon's face cracked in a smile as he sat on the edge of Shoshe's bed. The tiny girl seemed to disappear into the cushions, but the color had returned to her face and she no longer shivered from the fever.

"Who is that?" Her voice cracked.

"Aagon."

"I remember your voice."

"You were very sick last night. I was one of the men that helped care for you."

Shoshe's hand trailed towards the fresh bandages and Aagon's hand intercepted hers; squeezing it tightly. The girl turned her head to give Aagon a blind stare. "Will I ever see again?"

"Oh, don't think about that. We have some of the kingdom's best healers to help you."

"I was a healer too before... before all of this. I know that I'm hurt badly. I know that my eyes are broken."

Aagon gave a sigh. Despite everything that he had seen, all of the dead and wounded soldiers that he had seen piled in the hospital, nothing compared with the pain that he felt when sitting by this blind girl. Her entire life had been taken away in one violent stroke. Her family gone, her eyesight stolen, only her life remained. Even that might not last for long.

"The gods have a reason for everything," he began in a soft whisper, "their ways are mysterious and strange to us. No matter how much we suffer in this realm we will forget all of our pains in the next."

"I have been damned. The gods don't care about anyone anymore."

"Maybe you will see the purpose of your blindness someday."

"I don't want a purpose," Shoshe's voice filled with rage, "I want to see the Northerners dead."

Aagon rocked back at the bluntness of the girl's anger; the bandaged face remained devoid of any emotion, only the anger in her voice carried her true feelings. He suddenly felt uncomfortable and had the need to leave the room. "There are things I must take care of; I will have someone check on you later." Giving the girl one last pat on the hand Aagon rushed out. Emerging into the hallway Aagon nearly bumped into Seramin. From the look on Aagon's face the captain could see that not all had gone well.

"The girl is simply crushed by the loss of her eyesight. She says that the gods have abandoned her, and she talks of revenge against the Northerners," the priest explained before Seramin could ask.

"Who would blame her?" Hydrib retorted, his massive frame leaning against the wall. "She had everything going for her, then, gone like that." He snapped his fingers to accentuate the point.

"Every event in life is because of the gods, everything is a part of a greater plan." Aagon began to feel his own anger building up like steam.

"Trust me, priest, the gods are a bunch of children with sticks and we're the ants."

"What should we do about the girl?" Seramin asked, jumping between the two men before the fight escalated even more. Shoshe had refused to eat for several days, and had begun to fall into depression. It was as if she had lost the will to live.

"I really don't know what to do. The girl wants to die. She thinks that she has nothing left to live for. And, with the recent turn of events, I can see why."

"There has to be something!" Seramin's quivering voice revealing the growing fear. Aagon threw his hands up in defeat.

"You and I have both talked to her. It seems like the harder we try the more she resents life. Gods know what needs to be done!"

Hydrib released a loud moan and smashed his ham-sized fist into the wall, quieting the priest and the captain. "I'm tired of your wining. You want things fixed? I'll fix them for you!" Muscling his way past the two open-mouthed men the prisoner kicked in the door, and then proceeded to drag Shoshe from the bed by the arm. Too surprised to fight, the girl hung limp, her legs dragging over the floor.

"What are you doing?" Seramin screeched.

"It's time for a little tough love," Hydrib growled.

Thrashing and kicking her tiny legs Shoshe fought in vain to free herself from the giant's grip. "Let go!" Her screeching voice halted all movement in the hospital. Healers stopped in mid-spell, wounded quieted their moaning to hear the pleas of the girl, even the dead under their blankets of white seemed to take notice. Hauling Shoshe to the center of the wounded the prisoner shoved her roughly to the floor. She fell in a heap, knocking over a bucket of blood. Covered in the sticky liquid she began to cry when realizing what it was.

"Hydrib, stop this!" Aagon ordered sternly.

"Stay where you are, old man!" The priest jumped back as if physically slapped. Then, turning back to the girl Hydrib found another bucket of blood and proceeded to throw it on Shoshe, completely covering the girl in the fluid. "You want your eyesight back, here, take the blood that these men have spilled for you. They died for you. For you! People like you make me sick. You whine and cry when others hurt you, but do you do anything about it? No! You just curl up into a ball and cry.

"You want revenge? Start acting like you want it! Nothing good comes to those who do nothing. Bad things happen to all of us. But you don't see me crying about it." Hydrib surveyed the hospital which had grown deathly quiet during his rant. Only the dripping of blood could be heard as the crimson droplets fell from Shoshe's shaking body, splattered against the floor.

"Life's tough... Deal with it!" Hydrib marched out of the room, shoving his way past a flabbergasted Seramin and Aagon, muttering as he left, "I have."

Throwing open the door to the unforgiving winter, Hydrib took a deep breath, reveling at the hand that reached into his chest to grip his lungs. "To war, boys! A good amount of you will die tonight. I intend to live!"

Chapter 12
A Vision

The lands lying north of the capital city here wild and untamed. Rugged ice-covered mountains and miles upon miles of forest. Every once in a while a mighty river, or a timid stream, would disrupt the flow of green foliage, cutting a vein of striking blue blood into the earth's hard and unforgiving flesh. Lakes remained rare commodities, supplying those fortunate enough to live near them large quantities of fresh water and fish.

The south was an entirely different picture. Gone were the trees, and in their place miles upon of miles of prairie stood. Ponds and marshes dotted the landscape, giving living quarters for flocks of geese and ducks. Pheasants and prairie chicks hid among the grasses, living off of the seeds and scratching in the dusty ground for grains. Being rare in this part of the world trees became a measure of wealth. Those that could afford the higher taxes or the pressures of jealous neighbors sought out the few clusters of snow-white birches and gnarled oaks, building cozy homes of pine logs; cool and shady in the summer and protected from the fierce winds during the long winter months.

Shoshe found herself walking down a road that showed signs of misuse. Once a major highway to the city of Kelmdor, a farming city, the road was now full of potholes and patches of slippery ice. Kelmdor was a major producer of grains for the empire, but the war had marked other things as top priority. Not knowing where she was going the girl continued to navigate her way through the mud and patches of ice that filled the ruts. As she walked Shoshe glanced around at her surroundings.

Skinny cows and malnourished horses poked their heads out from their shelters, trying to see if this stranger would offer out any treats. A small present before the starving farmers butchered them for whatever nourishment their tough bodies could offer. Fields still stood untouched; long stalks of corn, wheat and barley poking up through the snow. Piles of hay lay scattered, not enough laborers had been present to bring the feed into barns for safekeeping. Livestock was forced to search for whatever they could find.

As the hours passed the landscape became more and more wild. Farmhouses rotted and fell apart. Animals lay dead in the fields, frozen solid. Carts sat solemnly by the roadside. Broken wheels and axles too expensive to repair. Some farms seemed as if they hadn't been worked for years. Shoshe became more and more worried. As the landscape fell into worse decay the threat of some unseen danger seemed to become stronger.

Then, just as the first shadows of night began to creep from their daytime dwellings, Shoshe rounded a final bend and saw a small house nestled amongst the snow, smoke puffing merrily out of its chimney.

Unable to find any trees of suitable size the owner had dug large grey stones from the fields and had constructed all four walls and chimney with stone and mortar. The roof was made of several solid wooden beams and sod cut from the ground like brown-green shingles. To the west of the house sat a barn just large enough to house three cows, a small family of pigs, and the family horse. To the south were the fields; the primary produce being wheat, corn, barley, and beans. The small family garden near the rear of the house housed a plethora of greens during the warm summer months; green beans, tomatoes, radishes, peppers, cabbage, carrots, and the occasional pumpkin or two in the summer. It now sat dormant and dead.

Shivering from the cold Shoshe hurried towards the house. Perhaps the people living there would be generous enough to give her some food. As she neared the building she began to have the feeling that something was not right. At the edge of the house were the corpses of three cows. The last had been killed only recently; the snow drenched in blood from the poor animal's death throes. The creature had been greedily hacked to pieces, chunks of meat ripped away from the ribs. The "butcher" had not even attempted to cut the meat properly.

Standing in the middle of the field Shoshe noticed for the first time that there were no people around, none. In the village there had always been a few farmers that braved the cold and ventured out to perform some task that could not wait for more favorable weather.

Shouts began to emit from the house. The cries of battle. Men's voices, some in pain, others in anger. A woman screamed, "Stop, stop!" Over and over again. Huddling behind the barn Shoshe waited as the sounds of the fight eventually ceased, growing dimmer until the only sound from the house was the loud wail of a child.

Not knowing why, Shoshe mustered up her courage and moved to the door. Dread seemed to float from the house like a bad draft. Looking down to the ground Shoshe saw a puddle of blood seeping out from under the door. Her stomach lurched at the sight. The red liquid made its way to the snow where it turned the pure powder into an ugly slop.

The crying of the child continued on, growing louder and louder. The sound pierced into Shoshe's soul and she ripped at the door, but it would not budge. She threw her full weight at the wood, but it still refused to open. Shrieking in rage Shoshe kicked at the door, pounding until her foot throbbed in pain. Throwing her arms down in disgust she noticed something lying in the snow.

A large brass key, untouched by snow, sat by Shoshe's feet. Grabbing the metal object she gasped as a strong burning sensation entered her fingertips as if the key had suddenly grown red hot. Inserting it into a lock that she had not noticed earlier Shoshe pushed the door open.

A burst of flame threw the girl backwards. Falling into the snow she covered her face as fire and smoke poured from the open door. Staggering out of the house came a man completely encased in fire. Instead of screaming in pain and collapsing on the ground the man reached a hand for Shoshe and began to advance towards her. Giving a scream the girl scrambled to her feet as the man drew closer.

Scrambling through the woods Shoshe recoiled as the burning man drew closer. His clothes had now long ago fallen from his frame. Now stripes of blackened skin began to peel from his bones and float away in the breeze like pieces of paper. Tripping over logs and forcing her way through bramble bushes Shoshe urged her legs to move faster.

Bursting from the forest Shoshe found herself facing a large city that burned fiercely in the night. An army of warriors attacked the walls with ladders and grappling hooks. The leader stood to the side, arms crossed over his chest as he watched the destruction of the fortress. For a moment Shoshe forgot about the fiery monstrosity that had been chasing her and watched awestruck as the forces assaulted the city, the defenders powerless to stop the onslaught.

A branch snapped and Shoshe whirled around, remembering what had chased her in the first place. The fire had completely consumed the flesh of the man, turning him into a burning skeleton. With a wide, toothy grin it reached a bony hand towards Shoshe's throat.

With a scream Shoshe lurched forwards, awakening from her nightmare. Her heart pounded in her chest and the sheets were tangled around her legs. Sweat poured down her face. Mopping her brow with the sleeve of her shirt Shoshe tried to calm her breathing. In the night a roar sounded as the Northerners attacked.

Chapter 13
Siege

Out of the shadows Northern warriors began to appear. Moving slowly, with shields raised to protect themselves they began to advance towards the fortress. They stepped carefully over the piles of dead and broken siege weapons that littered the ground. Hidden inside the trees archers began to launch volleys of arrows onto the heads of the defenders and the glow of sorcerers' spells could be seen as they began their chants.

"Loose!" an officer cried, giving the signal to forty archers on the stone wall.

Bowstrings hummed and arrows screamed through the air. Only a few found their targets, shields and heavy armor stopped most of the projectiles, and only ten barbarians fell to the ground. The archers were quick to react and soon their bows were once again fitted with arrows and another volley sent into the Northerners to thin the ranks once more.

A red glow blossomed from Aagon's hands as he summoned a fire ball. The spell hit a group of spearmen that had nearly reached the wall. Their screams were short-lived as fire entered their lungs and melted the thin tissue like wax. Waving their arms they danced in the firelight. Spells began to strike the fortress; small fireballs arched high into the sky and fell inside the walls like mortar shells, tongues of lightning crackled and scorched the stone and threw men backwards, and sparks fell from the sky burning skin and scorching clothes.

Taking up positions on the wall Seramin and Hydrib watched the agonizingly slow advance of the Northerners. A large number of portable wooden shields moved forwards in order to give protection to crossbowmen that stood and picked off defenders on the walls. Many of the warriors carried pieces of scrap wood and were dumping them at the base of the wall. Using wooden shields as cover they began to construct scaffolding that would allow them to climb quickly to the top of the wall.

Some of the soldiers threw rocks at the scaffolding, but they were too small and simply bounced off of the wooden shields. Hydrib disappeared from Seramin's side for a moment, and then returned lugging a large chunk of the wall that had broken off from an earlier attack. Tossing it over the side he grinned when he saw the scaffolding collapse in a heap of broken wood and crushed bodies.

"We must keep the barbarians from the walls!" Aagon ordered moving archers to a better position so that they could angle their shots behind the wooden shields. Seramin joined the rest of the defenders as they threw rocks and pieces of scrap wood over the side of the wall. Hydrib's boulders continued to crush the half-completed scaffolding, sending Northerners scurrying away like ants for the archers to find.

Trying a different tactic the attackers began lobbing pieces of burning pig fat with the small catapults they had labored to drag to the top of the mountain. The burning blobs hit the ground and burst in mushrooms of fire. Seramin dived to the ground as one of the burning balls whizzed past his head and struck an archer in the chest. The man erupted in flames and tipped over the edge. With the wall illuminated by fire the Northern archers took a terrible toll on the defenders of the fortress. The warriors surged once again.

Once three of the scaffolds had been completed the barbarians sent in their full attack. Bursting out into the light of the moon a massive wave of warriors sprinted to the wall. Arrows and Aagon's spells cut them down, but there were simply too many to stop. Ladders hit the wall and lines of Northerners began to charge up the scaffolding.

The first warrior to appear above the wall was quickly thrown backwards as Aagon's hammer crushed his skull. The priest was screaming prayers to the sun gods as he fought; throwing warriors to all sides as his mighty hammer swept them from the wall like a massive broom.

Seramin's twin blades spun in an impressive display of swordsmanship as he blocked off another ladder. Blood soon covered his shirt as more and more Northerners fell to his swords. He ducked under a swinging axe and kicked the man in the groin, tipping him over before stabbing him in the back as he fell. A flying mace struck a glancing blow to Seramin's arm, but the plate armor on his wrist deflected the blow and he spun in a quick circle and the mace, along with the hand that had been holding it, went spinning off into the night.

The defense held strong despite the arrows and spells that were falling on the Southerner's heads as an overwhelming number of warriors climbed up the scaffolding. Pike men blocked the tops of the ladders, hiding behind their shields while simply pushing men off to a crushing landing below. Archers shifted their fire to the bases of the ladders, hitting warriors that were too busy climbing to hold up their shields.

But, the defenders of the fortress were still taking casualties. Slowly, yet surely, the Northerners began grinding down their numbers and small breakthroughs developed as warriors managed to push past the first line of defense and make their way into the lower grounds. Dead and wounded from both sides covered the wall; the blood made the stones slick and slippery. The battle became a butchery as men hacked at each other with axes and swords.

Glancing to the side Seramin watched as the prisoner continued to increase the mound of dead barbarians before him. Standing atop a pile five deep he cut men in half and hacked off limbs with his sword. Blood covered his face and arms, and his mouth was twisted into an animal-like snarl; eyes wide and wild with blood lust.

Soon the unavoidable breakthrough developed as twenty warriors pushed their way over the wall and rushed into the courtyard. Seramin, Aagon, and several others flew down the steps in order to stop the enemy. Although outnumbering the Southerners, the warriors didn't stand a chance against Aagon's plethora of spells. An invisible force of magic pushed many of them back, throwing men against walls and snapping bones in half with the impact. A blue lightning bolt cut through four more, burning flesh and igniting clothes.

Seramin jumped into the fray, cutting down those that tried to flee from the priest. Nothing survived from the fury of his blades. When all of the warriors had been killed the captain turned to return to the wall when he saw Greot, tied to his pole. The orc was desperately yanking at his chains and cursing when they did not budge. Seeing Seramin's stare he stopped.

"Free me's! I can help," he growled lifting up his shackled hands to the human.

"If I do, will you betray us?"

"No." Greot shook his head. "I's will fight your's enemy. I's pledge my's loyalty to you's!"

The captain wavered as he thought about the offer. The defense needed every man that it could get its hands on, but what if the orc resorted back to its nature and attacked the defenders instead? Seeing Seramin's hesitation Greot growled softly, "You's needs me."

Having nothing to lose, and knowing that another fighting hand was needed, Seramin grabbed the keys from their nail and quickly released the orc. With great care Greot reached down and picked up an axe, testing the weapon's weight in his great green hands.

"Do not let me down, orc," Seramin ordered sternly as he turned and ran back to the battle.

"I's will not, human."

The orc proved himself to be a very capable soldier. His new axe was soon cutting down warriors as they hopped onto the wall. But, even with this new champion now fighting, the defense stood at the brink of collapse. Through the confusion of the battle Seramin suddenly found himself faced with a large warrior dressed in full plate armor. A helmet with two curved horns rested on his head. Armed with both a long sword and a spiked mace the man loomed over the captain. Ornate markings on the man's chest plate indicated a significant rank. Blackness hid inside the helmet's vision slits, giving Seramin the impression of an animated suit of armor before him.

For a second the two adversaries stood their ground, weapons raised and waiting for the other to make the first move. They both attacked at the same time.

Seramin's sword struck the leader's and he felt his arm give under the pure strength of the other man. The mace came spinning through the air, aimed at the captain's head, and he barely avoided the weapon. One of the spikes on the mace scratched his cheek and Seramin could feel hot blood squirting from the wound. The Northerner pressed the attack, pushing Seramin backwards as he tripped and stumbled over dead bodies. The mace was connected to a long chain and the warrior used this to his advantage, attacking Seramin at a distance.

Dancing from side to side in order to prevent himself from being hit by the spinning mace, Seramin could not launch a single attack of his own. Getting careless with his attacks the barbarian swung the mace horizontally where it crashed into the back of one of his own men, crushing his spine with a loud pop. The warrior hesitated, which gave Seramin the chance he needed. Thrusting low with a sword he aimed for the warrior's chest. In a loud crash and a shower of sparks the sword's blade broke apart as it contacted with the magically reinforced armor. The next thing that Seramin knew he was flying in the air as the warrior's fist connected with the side of this head. His limp body flew over the edge of the wall into the courtyard.

The stable broke his fall; punching through the wooden roof Seramin landed in a soft pile of hay. Then the stable collapsed, trapping him underneath.

Walking down the stairs the leader moved to the pile of wood that his enemy was trapped beneath. He doubted that the man had been killed by the fall and was looking to finish him off. Using his sword the leader pushed away pieces of the broken roof, looking to unearth Seramin.

Trapped beneath a heavy wooden beam Seramin could hear the barbarian as he drew closer. After the fall his swords had fallen from his hands and were nowhere to be seen. Straining against the beam he struggled to escape; he felt it give a little. Pushing with all his strength Seramin raised the beam another inch… then the warrior kicked aside a chunk of roofing and revealed the pinned captain.

The mace came down, ready to smash in Seramin's skull. Putting all of his strength into his legs Seramin pushed the beam up another half a foot, and into the path of the mace. The heavy metal ball smashed into the wood, cracking the old and weakened beam in half. Now free from his prison Seramin turned to face the warrior and barely managed to dodge the mace again.

"Human!" Greot screamed from the wall, axe in hand. With a mighty throw the orc sent the axe flying through the air towards the captain. The heavy weapon spun so fast in appeared to be a single rotating disc, but Seramin still managed to catch it and twirl around in time to stop the leader's sword. Dropping a hand to his boot Seramin pulled out a large hunting knife, jamming its blade into the knee of the enemy warrior. Overcome with pain the man lowered his sword slightly.

The opening gave Seramin the opportunity to drive the axe home. Axes are rather heavy and slow-moving weapons, but the momentum that they gain gives them the power to punch through even the thickest of armor. The blade cut deep into the warrior's arm as he raised it to save his head. As a reflex the warrior threw the mace forwards, hitting Seramin in the stomach and throwing him backwards.

The air exploded from his lungs. Seramin could barely stand from the pain that shot through his ribs. His armor had saved his life, but the impact from the mace had badly bruised his stomach. Struggling to his feet the captain used the stairs that led to the ramparts for support.

With an animal-like roar the warrior yanked the embedded axe from his left arm and threw it at the dazed Seramin, who jerked to the side. The axe clanged off of the stone in a shower of sparks. The warrior then reached to his knee and pulled the knife out as well. He made no cry this time, but the weapon made a sickening slurp as it pulled free.

Slow because of his wounds the warrior made to throw the knife at Seramin, but at that same moment the captain had also been in the process of throwing a dagger aimed at the leader's eyeholes in his helmet. The two blades clanged as they hit each other in midair.

Now out of weapons Seramin searched for anything that he may use to defend himself. A war hammer lay on the ground at Seramin's feet. He hefted the massive weapon with both hands, testing the weight. Weak from the loss of blood the man's sword was easily knocked aside by the hammer, and then Seramin swung the metal hammer into the warrior's helmeted head.

They clanged as the two chunks of metal hit. The man's head snapped back, blood shooting through holes in the helmet, and then it bounced back into place as if on a spring. Seramin hit him again, and again. He swung the hammer as hard as he could, but the warrior refused to go down. Every time his head would jerk to the side, but then it would move back to its original position.

Blood poured from the helmet now, running down to the front of the warrior's chest. He wavered, swaying to the side. Unable to swing the weapon again, fatigue gripping his arms, Seramin placed the hammer head to the man's chest and pushed. The warrior finally gave in to defeat and fell onto his back.

The battle was over. The Northerners had suffered terrible losses from the attack; their dead littered the field in front of the fortress, and made bloody piles on the scorched wall. The defenders had suffered equally. They had defeated the enemy, but their only reward was a fortress full of dead and wounded, and the knowledge that the enemy was still out there and that they would soon attack again. The attackers retreated to the trees in order to lick their wounds while the Southerners went through the grim process of collecting their wounded and finishing off the Northerners that still had breath in their lungs.

Aagon and Hydrib climbed down the stairs to meet with Seramin, who stood above the barbarian that was now beginning to twitch and jerk his healthy arm. The priest's blue and brown robes were tattered and bloodstained; a bloody gash bled furiously above his left eyebrow. The prisoner grinned evilly as he walked over the dead, not even giving the fallen the courtesy of stepping around their bodies.

With the last of his strength the warrior pulled the battered helmet from his head and tossed it to the side. He revealed a bashed and bloody face; his nose had been shattered by the blows from the hammer, and several of his teeth were now missing. The breath in Seramin's lungs failed him and he fell to a knee, trying hard to breathe.

"I's didn't betray you's," Greot said as he limped forwards, an arrow embedded in his right leg.

"No… you didn't," Seramin wheezed, giving a small smile of gratitude to the orc.

"What is he doing here?" Aagon asked angrily as he pointed to the orc.

"I released him… we needed the extra help." Seramin struggled back to his feet so that he could look the priest in the eye.

"Extra help yes, but not from the likes of him! I will not stand by as we ally ourselves with an abomination such as that!"

Taking a step forwards Greot clutched his newly acquired axe tightly. "I's kills the bad ones, and I's saves dis human."

"The creations of Kouja do not belong among our realm. You shall be cast back into the fiery pit of hell from which your disgusting race has come," Aagon spat.

"Orcs is much different than we's was."

"You'll never change. Evil never changes." The priest motioned for his men. "Put this creature back into its chains," he ordered.

The crowd of soldiers that had formed drew their weapons. Moving in on Greot their way became barred as Seramin jumped between them. "As captain of his majesty's royal army I order you not to touch him."

"Step down, Seramin, and allow me to establish the gods' will on this creature."

"This orc saved my life, and countless others tonight. No more innocent blood will be spilled here tonight."

Aagon gave a haggard laugh, coughed phlegm from his throat, and then spat the mess at Greot's feet. "No orc is innocent."

"That be true or not, I owe this orc my life tonight."

"Captain, have you fought in the campaigns against the orcs? Have you seen the atrocities that these creatures are capable of? Do you really want to take charge of this…thing?"

"Yes."

Giving a snort Aagon threw his arms up in defeat. Looking about the faces of the bloodied soldiers that surrounded him the priest calmed his breathing, waiting for his temper to cool. Whenever caught in an argument of religion his rage took the better of him. Now, after having lived through yet another assault by the Northerners, Aagon's patience was stretched to the breaking point.

Seramin took his eyes from Aagon and looked at the others. The soldiers had grown tired; tired of the killing, tired of the cold, tired of being tired. Hydrib eyed the argument with a cool eye, saying nothing, but waiting to see who would arise victorious. Greot, the orc whose life now lay in the captain's hands, relaxed his grip on the axe; a look of fatigue escaped the green-skin's ugly face.

"You have a strange following," the priest accused after the moment of silence. "A blind girl, an orc, and this man…" He pointed a finger at Hydrib, who feigned a look of shock. "I don't know what to think of him yet."

"I'll save you the trouble. I'm not one to be trusted. If the time proves right, I'll kill any one of you." The prisoner shot a venomous glance at the crowd. The men backed up a step to give him a wider birth.

"I've never met one such as you before," the priest growled. "Almost a heretic, yet not a follower of the dark gods. Your actions this night have proven that."

"I'm one of a kind."

"What's of the bad one's?" Greot asked changing the subject. Aagon's head twisted so fast Seramin thought that it would break, the priest's expression stuck somewhere between anger and confusion.

"Greot has a point," Seramin agreed. "While we argue amongst ourselves the Northerners are still out there. And they will be back soon."

The soldiers looked at each other, the same thought on their minds. Again? How much more can we endure? Aagon looked at his pitiful band with disdain. "We will hold. The sun gods are on our side, we will prevail." The soldiers' faces fell. Their doom seemed sealed.

"You may have the gods on your side, but unless the mighty hand of Jipniv or Motka comes down on the barbarians they're gonna run right over you tomorrow." All eyes turned to Hydrib as he spoke. "They know how weak you are. One more push and this fortress will be theirs."

"What do you suggest then?" The priest was in no mood to listen to advice, especially that from a man he did not trust in the slightest.

"We fall back, retreat to Thuringer. Our lives will be better spent elsewhere. Dying on this mountain will prove nothing."

125

"And I thought you were for honor!"

Hydrib spat on the warrior that Seramin had felled. Then, he placed the tip of his sword on the man's breastplate before pounding a meaty fist onto the hilt, driving the tip of the blade into the barbarian's heart. A small gurgle fell to a low whisper as a puddle of blood leaked out to mix with that of the countless others that flowed among the courtyard. "I'm for killing. And I can do that much better if I live."

Chapter 14
The Ice Maiden

The retreat from the fortress was emotional, yet uneventful. Gathering what little could be salvaged the Southerners fled just moments before the Northerners attacked the wall for the final time. Some shed tears for fallen comrades, their bodies still lying in a frozen pile waiting to be buried. Walking wounded limped along painfully. Any that could lend a hand helped the poor souls to move, but it remained clear that they would not live long. The path of retreat soon became marked with footprints and blood. Even before the burning outline of the fortress had disappeared from sight wounded had already fallen.

The remainder of the force was pitiful to see. Those that did not have one form of an injury or another could be counted on one hand while the wounded stretched off into the night; many would not be able to defend themselves if an attack fell on them. They could only lie in the snow and wait for death. Despite their laughable state every soldier, even the injured, carried armor and weaponry. They would not fall quietly under the barbarians. They would die proudly defending their empire. Even if they were forgotten by their fellow countrymen the mountain would always remember the sacrifices of the Southern troops, dying far from home and far from loved ones.

Seramin trotted slowly, falling into the long-practiced retreat. His mind focused on his own loved ones, he did not notice the cold that stung at him, or the itch of his wounds that had already begun to heal due to his unknown power. Greot had taken the lead, not out of bravery, but because of the humans' distrust of him. Many had threatened to kill the orc if he made so much as a wrong move. The unknown of the mountain seemed to be more welcoming to Greot than the company of men. The orc had made his point very clear that he was to travel with the group now that he had a debt to pay for Seramin releasing him. Aaron had snorted at this. "An orc that fights for honor!" he said.

Aagon moved among the wounded, offering prayers to the gods while Hydrib fell into his own world, passing by those that asked for help. He did not bat an eye at those that pleaded and wept in desperation.

Mounted on one of the few remaining horses, Shoshe's body bounced up and down as the beast moved jerkily, led by a soldier that clutched the reins loosely, as if it did not matter if he let go and the horse, along with its passenger, stumbled off to their deaths. At first the girl had been frightened about the prospect of riding a horse, but after some coaxing Seramin had finally managed to persuade her to mount it.

"Do not be afraid, Shoshe, it is only an animal."

"It may be just an animal, but it's a lot bigger than me," she squeaked, "and I have never ridden a horse before."

"Well, this is the perfect time to learn."

Reaching down with an arm he hoisted the girl onto the saddle with him and began trotting the animal around, giving her the feel of a horse. After a few moments Shoshe giggled with delight.

"Reminds me's of my's child," Greot had remarked absentmindedly.

Seramin gave the orc a surprised look. "You have children?"

"Yes, one's girl of seven's years." The orc beamed.

"She have a name?"

"Layo."

"Pretty name, what does it mean?"

"It's doesn't mean anything's," Greot said simply, "it's just her name's."

"Oh…"

Once Shoshe was comfortable with riding a horse Seramin gave a command to the next ranking officer of the fortress, which was a pitifully low rank, and the gates opened a crack as to let them through. The dead from the other day had frozen stiff from the cold, locked in grotesque positions of death. A light blanket of snow had fallen during the night and a cloth of white partially hid the dead.

Now Shoshe was on the verge of sleep. She tipped dangerously to one side, but a green hand pushed her back into the saddle. The soldier that had been holding the reins jerked when he saw Greot and gave a scowl. The orc just returned the gesture with a tusked smile and waddled away.

They made good time for the first three days, pushing themselves along the road that wound its way through the mountain passes. Years of work when the kingdom had been united had built the series of roads that made travel through the mountains possible. Ancient trees had been felled and tunnels had been carved through solid rock. Now, years later, the Southern kingdom owned all of this work which had been stolen from the North during the beginnings of the great civil war.

On the fourth day of the retreat Aagon came to a halt and pointed to a forbidding mountain that now peeked out from its veil of mist, and snow, and ice. It towered over its neighbors and was twisted and crooked like an old hag. The left side of the mountain was devoid of snow from the winds that had exposed the rock beneath. Trees only grew at the base of the mountain; the rest of the peak devoid of life. "That mountain peak is the Ice Maiden, the haunted mountain."

The others shivered as they recalled the tales of the evil mountain. Legend told of ghosts that haunted the caves, searching for any soul unlucky enough to venture close. If the stories were to be believed, entire legions of soldiers had disappeared in the woods near the base of the mountain. None had survived. No sane man wandered any closer than necessary.

No one spoke now because the road fell into disarray and eventually became a tiny path, the trees pressed close like living things. The air grew colder, and the wind never stopped blowing through the valleys. Shadows jumped and twisted, giving them the appearance of monsters. There was the ever-present noise of creatures scurrying between the branches and the group soon had the feeling that they were being watched by something that was not entirely human.

The stories of the Ice Maiden had become so haunting that even the army refused to take this route. No longer in use the road ceased to exist. Piles of boulders and sheer rock cliffs pushed the survivors closer to the mountain. They didn't know what was worse, the Northerners behind them, or the ghosts that awaited in the mountain. They just pulled together and kept a careful watch. The worst of times came at nightfall, when unseen things scurried about in the night, just out of the campfires' light.

"The ghosts," Aagon stammered.

"These are ghosts that make footsteps," Seramin pointed out.

"True, the sound of their steps can be heard, but what do we truly know about ghosts?"

During the nights when the group made camp the fire refused to burn brightly and the wind tried its best to put it out. This is when the noises became worse. Heavy breathing and groaning floated out from the woods. From the Ice Maiden bloodcurdling screams sounded. Hydrib shouted at the noises, waving his sword about and taunting whatever was out there to come and face him, but nothing would. Soon everyone was suffering from sleep loss and dark rings sat under their eyes.

Aagon grew more and more paranoid. "The ghosts are toying with us; it will be only a matter of time before they descend upon us!"

Deeper into the woods they came upon a startling find. An expedition had made their way to the Ice Maiden years ago, but they had not made it. Skeletons of fallen soldiers littered the woods; hundreds of them, frozen in the ice. Weapons were scattered everywhere; spears broken and shields shattered.

Every tree was filled with bits and pieces of bones that hung from lengths of rope, even a few complete skeletons hung there as well. The heads had been severed from many of the dead and had been stacked into small mounds near unholy articles.

"What could have done this?" Hydrib asked as he picked up one of the skulls before tossing it aside.

"Ghosts!" the orc snarled gripping his axe.

"Then it would be ghosts that wield weapons." Seramin pointed to a series of skulls that had been shattered with what could have been a mace.

"This place is evil," Shoshe whispered. "I can hear the howling of the dead."

Everyone stopped to listen. Sure enough, cries and warnings could be heard in the wind. The ghosts were screaming at the intruders that had broken their rest. Hydrib simply laughed at them, but the others crowded together and began to draw their swords. The horses whined and tried to pull away.

"What's the matter, afraid of ghosts?" the prisoner laughed.

The priest's face turned beet red. "What is wrong with fearing the unknown?"

"Trust me, old man; there are worse things in this world than ghosts."

"What could be worse than a ghost?" Shoshe asked. One of the bloodcurdling screams sounded. She squeaked in fright and ducked behind Seramin.

"We may soon find out."

As they drew closer to the Ice Maiden the group came upon more and more of the grisly scenes, some of them dating back many years from the appearance of the weapons and armor. The ghosts grew louder in the night while the crooked mountain grew taller. Many of the soldiers wanted to retrace their steps and find a different way around the mountain, but in the distance hundreds of Northerners marched to the south. Either naïve or unknowing of the ghosts they did not show any hesitation in their advances.

"We will reach the base of the mountain tomorrow," reported Aagon as they began to make camp. "One more day and we will begin to put this place behind us."

"What if we don't last that long?" one of the few remaining soldiers, a boy no older than nineteen, asked nervously. "The ghosts have granted us mercy thus far, but they will soon kill us!"

"Ghosts won't hurt us," Seramin scolded with a shake of his head.

"You don't believe in the undead, even after what you've seen?" the youth asked incredulously.

"I only believe in what I can see."

The sun was setting fast in the north and it was growing even colder than before. Several of the men set out to light a fire.

"We have still seen no ghosts," Seramin remarked.

"They are waiting for the opportune moment," Aagon said.

"Why? They seemed to have killed off those heavily armed bands without any trouble. Why would the ghosts not finish us off quickly?"

"It may be best not to ask that question and just thank the sun gods that we have made it this far."

Shoshe knelt beside the tiny fire and began to throw on sticks, finding the flames by feeling for the heat. In a few minutes the heat that grew from the yellow and orange tongues was enough to warm her chilled bones. Greot dropped a load of logs by her side, and then knelt down to put them on the fire.

"There is no need for you to do that, I can manage," Shoshe said softly.

"It no problem for's me's," the orc said quickly. "I's want to help."

Shoshe smiled as the orc threw the wood on the fire before leaving abruptly. *How sweet, an orc that cares about me,* Shoshe thought.

While arranging furs on the ground for a bed Seramin felt a presence behind him. Turning he faced Aagon; the priest cocked his head toward Shoshe. "Look at them," he whispered in a barely audible tone.

Greot returned from the woods with another armload of wood. Throwing the wood beside the fire he sat next to the girl. Shoshe laughed as they chatted as if old friends. Greot even smiled, if you could call the face that his hideous features made a smile. "The orc is getting too close to the girl."

"I don't know, he seems harmless enough."

"I never will trust that creature, but that is beside the point. I have other things to discuss with you."

"Like what?" The captain finished positioning the furs and began to build a fire of his own.

"Hydrib."

"What about him?" he asked with some hesitation. Seramin did not want to discuss any particulars about the prisoner, but now it seemed as if he had no choice; the priest was determined to drag some information out of him.

"Do you not feel uneasy about that man? It seems as if there is an aura about him, something evil. His eyes are always wandering, studying our moves, calculating. I don't trust him."

"It seems to me that you don't trust anyone, Aagon."

"It's not just that. Have you taken a look at the man's sword?"

Twisting around Seramin squinted until the bulk of the prisoner came into view. The man sat in the snow, back leaning against a small tree. The black weapon lay over his lap. "It is big, but—"

"Can you read the runes?"

"Well, no," Seramin admitted shaking his head.

"Well, neither could I, but before abandoning the fortress I consulted some of the older scripts and found a translation." Digging into a pocket the priest revealed a crumpled piece of parchment. "The language is old, older than any other known by the Guild of Priests, but several scriptures still exist. I translated the runes from these works."

Seramin hated the suspense. "What does the sword say?"

"It says 'gehinem.'"

"What exactly does that mean?"

"It doesn't mean anything, it's a name."

"A name?" Seramin gave a puzzled look as he registered the information.

"Yes, a name, although I didn't know that until further research. That was when I found this." He motioned to the paper clutched in one hand. "This is a page from *Silia Aries*, a chapter of the *El Inu's Esnt'a*. The sun gods' most holy bible."

Unfolding the paper Aagon began to read. "'And as the sun gods ascended into the heavens they told the inhabitants of the earth to guard the secrets of the past, so that the evil ones did not rise again. All secrets of the world shall be placed beneath the ground, never to be unearthed again. Sinji and Kouja shall remain in the underworld and they shall never walk the earth again. Protection of the *Kirahs* is all important;

they shall never be uncovered by the evil ones. So it was told, and so it was done.'"

The pair sat in silence, allowing the information to sink in. Seramin stole a glance at Hydrib, looking at the shadowy hulk as if to glean the information from him. There was so much that he did not know about the prisoner; what else could the man be hiding?

"So, what exactly what does gehinem mean?"

"It's the Elvish name for fire. But, the real question is what is a man doing carrying a weapon inscribed with an ancient language older than the race of humanity itself?"

"Yes," Seramin agreed, "and what are the Kirahs?"

A low growl rumbled in the darkness. Turning slowly Shoshe searched for the source of the noise. It was very close. In a flash of snapping twigs a black shape leapt onto her, putting out the fire when a foot kicked the burning logs into the snow. Shoshe screamed.

"Shoshe!" Hearing the girl's screams Seramin pulled out his swords and raced to the two figures that grappled in the snow, rage burned in his heart as a small animal growl came from his throat. His teeth bared Seramin raised a sword and prepared to drive it into the creature that was laying on Shoshe... then was knocked down by another creature that barreled into him from the side.

More of the black shapes ran into the camp, hacking and slashing at the unprepared soldiers. Dozens of the black shadows materialized from the darkness, pulling men to the ground before dragging them away into the darkness. Their victims screamed as they disappeared.

"Ghosts!" screamed Aagon as he summoned a spell that illuminated the night in a flash of blinding light. Howls of agony sounded as the creatures raised their arms to cover their eyes, shrieking with rage they ran blindly towards the priest. Ducking below outstretched claws he swung his hammer, hitting one of the creatures, splitting its chest wide open. Spots of hot liquid squirted onto Aagon's cheek. The creatures bled! They could be killed! Seeing that the foes he faced were tangible and killable the priest's courage rejuvenated.

Jumping out from the shadows, armed with cruel spears and clubs fashioned from tree limbs, the monsters swung wildly at the few hardened fighters that remained. Standing within the protection of Aagon's illumination spell the Southerners cut down the monsters. The creatures had incredible strength, but their attacks were untrained and easy to block.

Shoshe managed to push her attacker away and began to crawl away from the snarling beast, but a pair of strong hands grabbed her by the anklets and yanked her back down, and then, her arms waving frantically, the girl was pulled away into the forest.

"Shoshe!" Seramin cried as he watched helplessly. The trail in the snow could still be seen in the dim light of the moon and he jumped into the woods, following the sound of snapping sticks as the monsters carried away their prize.

Overwhelmed by the beasts' numbers the defense crumbled. Separated and cut off the men were hunted down and killed to a man. Aagon and Greot found themselves fighting back to back in the corpse-strewn camp. The orc's axe severed limbs while the priest's hammer crushed rib cages and decapitated heads.

Animal-like snarls and shrieks sounded with each contact that the pair's weapons made, sinking deeply into the mangy fur, or else crushing muscle into pulpy goo. As the spell faded away, and the last of the white rays were defeated by the darkness the wave of monstrous creatures ceased. As soon as it had begun the attack ended and silence returned to the haunted forest once again.

Aagon rubbed at his eyes to get out the thick stream of blood that had came from a severed vein. The liquid burned like fire and he wanted to gouge out his own eyes in order to rid himself of the feeling.

"Where's is Seramin?" Greot asked; he held his arm tightly which had been cut from one of the shoddy spears.

A distant scream from Shoshe told them all that they needed to know. Aagon finished rubbing the blood from his eyes and looked around; the lumps of the dead covered the ground, and turned the snow black with spilt blood. "The creatures have the girl!"

"Seramin's must have followed's."

"With these creatures filling the woods there will be no chance of finding them."

Greot looked around, something else was missing. "Where Hydrib?"

Aagon groaned; they had lost him as well? A quick check of the bodies confirmed that Hydrib had survived the battle and was somewhere in the woods. Howls in the distance discouraged the priest and the orc from remaining at the campsite and waiting for morning. Picking up their weapons they set off in search of Seramin and Shoshe; Aagon led the way, no longer as afraid now that he knew that the enemy that he faced could be killed, but still cautious of the ally that trotted by his side.

Besides the screams and howls of the monsters in the distance the woods remained dead silent. Nothing moved, and the moon gave only just enough light for them to see things that were less than two feet in front of them. Neither Aagon nor the orc was skilled at tracking, and the trail soon became lost and they resorted to walking in the general direction of the mountain in hopes of running across Seramin and the girl.

A bush shook as a body rubbed against it. The priest and the orc froze and drew their weapons, doing their best to look into the darkness and find what was fallowing them. They both shook, but stayed just the same, ready to meet the attack if more of the monsters charged them. The woods remained silent, however, and they grew more and more worried.

A hand slid out from behind Aagon and closed over his mouth. "Mwhp!" he cried as the strong hand yanked him backwards.

"Silence!" a familiar voice hissed.

"Hydrib!" Greot exclaimed.

"Hdrb?"

The prisoner released Aagon and pushed him face first into the snow. "You two breathe so loud it's surprising that those monsters haven't found you already!"

"The beasts, they have Shoshe!" The priest spat snow out from his mouth and gasped for breath.

"I know, and the fearless captain is chasing them to their lair."

"We's must help's them!"

Hydrib shook his head slowly. "Probably a waste of time, but Seramin is still alive and this damned collar forces me to serve him. Right now he orders me to come to his aid." He grabbed at the piece of metal that hung around his neck and gave a yank, but it remained firm.

"What's so special about the collar?" Aagon asked trying to take a closer look at the magical item. Hydrib turned around before he had a chance.

"Let's go, the sooner we find Seramin the sooner I can stop this damn burning in my neck." He stomped off towards the Ice Maiden. Not wanting to be left behind, the other two followed.

Chapter 15
Into the Lion's Den

He ran until his chest felt as if it was to burst, but the screams of Shoshe gave the captain the motivation that he needed to keep going. Branches lashed at his face, cutting tiny lines of bleeding and torn flesh, and stumps leapt from the snow to bang into his knees. Gasping for breath Seramin charged out of the woods and began to make his way up the rocky side of the Ice Maiden.

The snow was deep and the trail of Shoshe and her captors was easy to follow; they had cut a straight path through waist-deep snow. For several minutes the captain scrambled up the rocks until his fingers bled and his elbows had become raw from the rigid stone. A primal anger inside of his heart grew bigger, giving him the strength and rage to make his way over the obstacles. The fatigue in his legs lessened, and his breathing came easier.

Rounding the bend Seramin came to a stop, amazed at what stood before him.

Carved into the side of the mountain itself were seven towering pillars that measured at least twenty feet in diameter. Supported by the pillars, a small ridge held a small army of stone carvings; man-sized monsters stood, looking down at Seramin with horrible sneers and silent cries of pain and torture. Behind the pillars a deep blackness appeared, signifying the existence of an entrance into the side of the Ice Maiden.

The trail ran up the multitude of stone steps that led to the pillars. Shoshe's screams were gone, but a sinking feeling in Seramin's stomach told him that she was now inside the mountain. Now taking caution against the monsters he walked up the stone steps, his eyes fixed on the entrance that looked more like a gaping mouth than anything else.

From above, Seramin couldn't see the stone carvings as they twisted their heads and watched as he walked below. Some flexed their clawed hands and growled softly, but they did not attack. These were not the creatures that defended the temple, there were greater horrors within. These statues only stood watch over the temple, witnesses throughout the millennia.

The hole led to a long, dark cave that wound to the left. Making a torch Seramin made his way inside the mountain. He did not know how far he traveled, or for what amount of time, but the captain could feel that the tunnel was gradually leading him downwards. The walls were rough and unworked, the ceiling barely tall enough for him to walk without bending his head. Despite his great care to remain quiet Seramin's footsteps thudded against the stone and echoed inside the mountain. He gritted his teeth against the noise and continued on, the torch in one hand and a sword in the other.

* * * * *

"Are you sure that this is the right way?"

"I'm sure!"

"I's don't think you's are."

"The collar doesn't lie, I know where to go!"

"What is the power of this collar? Is it magical?"

"Greot no like magic."

"Shut up, both of you! If either of you two utters so much as one more word I'll put your heads on a pike!"

"Sorry."

Kneeling to examine a footprint in the snow Hydrib gave a sniff. "Seramin came this way, this print came from his boot." There was something else next to the footprint and he leaned closer to get a better look.

"What is it?" Aagon asked nervously, his eyes darting to and fro. The beasts could return any second. The closer they drew to the mountain the lower his courage fell.

"It's a hoof print, like that of a horse or a mountain sheep."

"The monsters ride horses?"

"I don't think so; it's nothing like I've ever seen before."

When the trio came in sight of the pillars Aaron and Greot's mouths fell open in wonder while Hydrib simply glared.

"This must be a temple of some kind," the priest murmured.

"A temple to what god?"

"I don't know; it doesn't have any of the markings that would tell to what god it belongs to. Perhaps if we get closer I will be able to tell."

"This temple have's the girl then?"

"Yes, and Seramin too."

"Girl or not, those monsters have been using this temple as a den." Hydrib pointed to the series of hoof tracks leading to and from the opening.

"We must go in and help Seramin."

"Yes, and we's must help's the girl."

"Probably dead by now."

* * * * *

Shoshe remained still, frozen in fear as she heard the beasts stumbling around the chamber, their hoofed feet clicking loudly against the stone. They snorted and sniffed at her body, growling deep in their throats whenever she moved. They had pulled her arms around a pole set in the ground and had tied her wrists together. The rough rope burned her skin and she could feel the circulation to her hands being cut off. Her head ached from a painful bump she had received as the beasts had dragged her through the cave. She felt warm blood trickle down the side of her face. Pain pounded against the side of her skull. The feeling nearly drove her to tears.

Two soldiers had been dragged from the camp and now found themselves here with Shoshe. One whimpered somewhere in the far corner of the chamber while a second reprimanded the first.

"Shut up now, ya hear?" he hissed.

"They're gonna kill us," the first sobbed loudly.

"They will if you keep blabbering like that."

A roar cut the conversation short. One of the monsters hobbled over to the pair, smelling the humans with its nose. A tongue whipped over its lips, smacking noisily. "P-please don't kill me," the man whispered, fear dripping from his voice.

Giving a loud screech the monster threw itself at the crying man. The screams echoed inside the mountain as the creature's teeth bit down into the man's throat. More of the beasts crowded around the feast, scrambling for a bite of flesh. His screams finally disappeared as death took the man, but not before the crunching of bones could be heard.

Please, Seramin, hurry and help me. I don't want to be here, I want to go home! I'm scared. The pounding in her head intensified a hundredfold. Even though blind Shoshe saw red spots appear before her.

* * * * *

The main tunnel began to branch off in several directions, but a flickering light in the distance acted like a beacon, leading Seramin to his right. He heard clicking from the beasts' hooves as they paced back and forth. A man's screams had just ended. The unlucky fellow had lived for a long time before dying. The rage began to build up again inside the captain's chest as if it was a being that lived inside him and was trying to burst out. Putting out the torch he quietly armed himself with his other sword and made his way to the light. That was where Shoshe was, he just knew it.

As he ran, Seramin concentrated on the prisoner that wore another collar much like his own. "Prisoner, find me. I need your help."

* * * * *

Hydrib jerked to a sudden halt causing Aaron and Greot to run into his back, creating a bottleneck in the tight tunnel. He began clawing at his throat, swearing softly.

"What is wrong?" the priest asked as he untangled himself from the flailing arms of the orc.

"The collar, it's burning me!" The man pointed to the collar and sure enough, a thin trail of smoke was beginning to rise.

"What that's mean's?" Greot asked nervously.

"It means that the captain is stronger than I thought."

* * * * *

Emerging into the small cavern Seramin let out a roar that caused the monsters to jump. They all stood on two long, crooked legs with knees that were reversed like that of a dog. Dirty brown fur hid the thick layers of muscle that lay beneath. The heads of the beasts were the most hideous feature. Many had large gaping mouths filled with broken, yellowed teeth; long, pink tongues slapping at the air. Some had curved horns like a ram, some had deer antlers, still others had the horns of a bull.

The first beast never had a chance to move; one of the captain's swords cut its clawed arm. Blood pooled onto the floor as the creature squirmed and writhed. The next one was faster to react and managed to bring its spear up to block the next downward slash, but the rotten shaft snapped and Seramin's second blade dug deep into its belly.

Without flinching the creature accepted the fatal wound and set upon Seramin with its claws, cutting into his chest and leaving four long, bloody gashes across the left side of his face. Bringing the other sword up to protect himself Seramin cut off both of the creature's hands and pushed it away from him. Rivers of crimson flowed down his face, obscuring his vision.

There were still three of the horned creatures in the room, and now they had become wary of this new enemy. It was wounded, but had proven that it could still strike back. One beast armed itself with a club while the other two had simple wooden spears with sharpened ends.

"Seramin?" Shoshe called.

"It's me, I'm here."

"I knew you would come for me!"

The captain's mind was reeling. He had to think quickly and stall for time so that Hydrib could come and find him; he was sure that the prisoner would since the collar had forced him to come along on the journey this far, and it had already proven its powers to the captain at Talron.

"Can you free yourself from your bonds?"

"Maybe, I can try." Shoshe began to wiggle against the rope.

The beasts began to circle around Seramin, trying to box him in against the wall. He moved around with them, jumping out of their trap. He had to keep them lined up with his right eye; his left had now filled with blood and had become useless. Just a few more minutes… Just a few more…

Reaching the body of the handless beast the one with the club reached back with its hoofed foot and kicked the corpse at Seramin. Not expecting the flying body the captain was struck a glancing blow and thrown backwards against the cavern wall. The two spear-wielding monsters bore in on him, swinging their weapons with thick arms that looked like they could crack a tree in half. He managed to back away from the attacks while decapitating one with a double-bladed slash, and then turned the other one into a living fire when he kicked a torch from the ground, sending it flying against the beast's chest.

While he had been busy with these two Seramin had failed to notice the third monster, which had snuck around the room and had begun to put out the torches one by one until the only light in the cavern was that of the smoldering corpse, and that was quickly becoming weaker.

As it turned out the beasts had excellent night vision and the monster danced on either side of Seramin as he struck out in vain at the noise its hooves made. The club smashed into Seramin's arm, knocking a sword loose. Cursing he twirled around and slashed blindly at the attacker, but the beast had jumped aside and moved to a new position. The next blow struck Seramin square on the chest; he felt a rib crack as he fell down, his last sword clattering to the ground. Clicks echoed in his ears as the beast made its way closer, its club no doubt raised above its horned head and ready to deliver the final blow.

Where is Hydrib? Where is he? I need him!

A screech forced Seramin to clamp his hands over his ears as the beast ripped the very air with its piercing scream. Then, for a moment, it became silent and only a tugging sound, as if someone was punching a knife through cloth, could be heard, and then the beast gave a gurgling noise and fell to the ground.

The next thing that Seramin knew he felt the soft hands of sweet Shoshe grabbing his face. His mind swam from his wounds. For a moment he didn't even know where he was, but then everything came rushing back to him at once.

"Are you okay?"

"No," he let out a groan, "it's my ribs. How…how did you kill it?"

"With your sword."

"No, I mean, how did you find it? You're blind."

"I can see now."

"What?" Seramin didn't understand; he must have heard the girl wrong. What she said was clearly impossible.

"I can see now, as if it was daylight in here."

"How can you see? Your eyes are—"

"Gone?" she finished for him. "They are, but something has happened to me. It must have been the bump on my head, or possibly a gift from the gods. I can somehow see even though I have the cloth around what remains of my eyes and it's pitch black in here."

"Well, if you can see, can you take a look at my face? Those beasts hurt me pretty bad."

With great care Shoshe tilted the captain's head to the side and looked at the claw marks. "They aren't deep, you're just bleeding a lot because it's a head wound. I'm more worried about your chest."

"I'm fine, I've had worse."

"I know, but I heard the rib crack myself. It will be difficult for you to breathe, much less fight with it."

"Well, you said yourself that I heal fast, maybe I will again." He gave a smile in the darkness.

"I see," the blind girl said.

* * * * *

"Shoshe!" Greot roared as he and the other two charged into the chamber, weapons drawn and torches waving in the air. He stopped when seeing the dead beasts lying on the floor, and a pair of half-eaten soldiers tied to posts. The orc then saw Seramin and the girl sitting on the floor, waiting for their arrival.

"It's about time that you three showed up." Seramin laughed.

Hydrib screamed in rage, "You nearly burnt me to a crisp and all you can do is laugh? Why couldn't you have died and saved me the trouble?"

"I would have died if it hadn't been for Shoshe, she saved my life."

"Huh?"

"She can see now," Seramin explained. "Somehow, through magic, she can see again."

"Magic? Me's confused. Girl's has magic now?" The orc scratched his head.

"But, how?" Aagon stroked his beard, contemplating the phenomena.

More beasts released their humanlike screams that echoed down the tunnels. Hydrib raced down one of the five paths that led away from the chamber to find the threat, he returned quickly with a surprised look on his face.

"More monsters?"

"A lot more."

"We can discuss Shoshe's miracle at a later date." Seramin groaned as he pulled himself to his feet.

More screams echoed down the tunnel that led to the temple's entrance; their escape was blocked off. Seramin picked a different tunnel and began to hobble away; the rest of the group quickly followed without a word. The tunnel turned and changed directions without warning, its height and width drastically changing from a comfortable size to a nearly claustrophobic crushing feeling. In some of the places Hydrib barely had enough space to squeeze his massive frame through, but he grunted and groaned and managed to keep going.

They emerged into another cavern filled with a number of carvings of daemons, and several stone houses that had been built right inside the mountain. From their appearance they seemed to serve as guard houses to keep intruders from entering the small doorway that stood on the opposite side of the chamber. Several beasts stood in front of a fire, roasting pieces of meat on long sticks. They grabbed for their weapons, but a few of Aagon's fire bolts sent them scurrying away.

Moving through the doorway that was now broken open, two heavy slabs of granite that Aagon said were once magically shielding, according to the runic symbols on the sides, the group emerged into another cavern that dwarfed the other that they had just come from.

On the side of the cavern a small waterfall flowed, bursting out from the seemingly solid rock face. The water gathered in a deep pool before flowing over the edge and moving across the chamber and disappearing into the other wall. The river of water flowed into a deep moat that protected a massive wall made of solid stone. Measuring thirty feet in height the wall was complete with two guard towers and a wooden drawbridge that had long ago rotten away. All around the cavern small holes protruded from the walls; small barriers of stone had been built near these holes so that archers could hit an attacking force from every possible angle as the wall became under siege.

"What is this place?" Shoshe breathed, taking in the magnificence of the fortress with her newfound sight.

"Whoever built this place went through great lengths to keep this temple protected. The magically shielded door and this wall must be just two of several defenses that were built in order to keep intruders out," Aagon explained.

"But how do we get past the wall?" Seramin grumbled.

The screams were coming closer. The beasts hit the walls with their weapons and let the sound ring throughout the tunnels; war hammers banged as they drew closer. There must have been hundreds of them. But that was not the worst news to come. All along the stone wall shapes appeared as hundreds of beasts came out of hiding, daring the invaders of their home to attack. The holes in the walls now filled with monsters as well, these ones armed with crude bows and throwing spears. The band had been trapped.

There must be something, Seramin thought desperately. *Another tunnel or a secret passageway that we can go through.* He looked at the waterfall; the hole that it sprung from was too high to reach, and the force of the water would be too great to swim through. His gaze then switched to the other side of the cavern where the water disappeared through the wall. The rock had been worn away from years of erosion and the opening now rose to a height of two feet, just big enough for a person to crawl through. It wasn't much, but it could be just enough to get them out of harm's way.

The adjacent cavern lit up from numerous torches as the army of beasts appeared. Moving impossibly fast on their hoofed foot they moved to the open doorway in only a few short seconds.

"Follow me!" Seramin ordered, and then peeled off as fast as he could.

Archers in the holes fired and spears rained down from the air. Hydrib used the width of his blade as a makeshift shield and knocked the projectiles out of the air as he ran. Aagon fired bolts of lightning at the beasts, and also created a magical shield around the group that knocked the arrows off target. But, the beasts from the other cavern were closing fast. In a few more seconds they would be upon them.

Seramin reached the hole first. "Quick, inside!"

Without hesitating Shoshe dropped to her hands and knees and crawled out of sight. Hydrib was next, followed by Aagon, Greot, and then Seramin. The screams and growls grew louder, but the beasts stopped short of the tunnel, refusing to squeeze into such a tight space. Seramin breathed a sigh of relief, and then followed the others as they scurried away as fast as they could.

* * * * *

Churning his powerful legs through the deep snow Pouja worked his way to the cluster of warriors that guarded the entrance of the cave. All four instantly snapped to attention at the sight of their leader. Without noticing their salutes the king surveyed the surrounding area. Snow had begun to fall, filling the air with a thick sheet of white

147

powder. Trees pressed up against the mountain, but stopped in their tracks upon reaching the base of the Ice Maiden. Boulders the size of a house lay strewn about as if the gods themselves had carelessly tossed the massive objects about.

The entrance to the temple shivered behind the wall of snow, attempting to hide its presence from the Northerners. Numerous steps led to the small, dark opening that opened to the oblivion within. Releasing his breath Pouja watched as it crystallized in the air. Only the crinkling of the falling of snow against his shoulders could be heard. He sent a glance up to the top of the pillars, carefully examining the stone figures that glared down at him and his men.

Giving a small smile behind his helm the king of the North clenched a gauntleted fist in anticipation. The Southern fortresses had proven to be stubborn defenses, and had delayed the army's advance for several days, but the defenders had finally cracked and fled into the forest. Bursting through the gap his warriors hunted down the weaklings. But it appeared that they were not needed. The remains of a camp had been found, all of the men slain. The white flakes from the sky covered the bodies, giving the only burial that they would receive.

Zigmon trudged through the snow, breaking the peace that Pouja had been enjoying. The king gave a scowl, but then his features softened as the colonel arrived at his side. "Is all prepared?"

"Yes, my lord, the men have assembled and await your orders."

"Excellent. Give the word to begin searching the tunnels. We will find the object that rests in the mountain's bowels before long."

"Yes, of course…but—"

"Yes?"

"Well, my lord, the men speak ill of this mountain. Some even go as far as to say that it is haunted."

"Haunted?" The king laughed. "Why do they think that?"

"The destroyed Southerner camp has made the men nervous. There is a sign of a struggle, but there appears to be no sign of any attackers. No tracks, no blood trails, and no bodies."

"The snow could have easily covered their tracks, Colonel."

"Yes, my lord, please forgive my bluntness, but I have a bad feeling about this mountain."

"Surely you don't believe in ghosts?" Pouja laughed again, a rattling booming noise that sounded more like coughing. Zigmon quickly shook his head.

"Perhaps not ghosts, but there are things in this world that have never been discovered, and should not be discovered—"

"Have you lost faith in our cause?" a voice cooed softly. Zigmon turned around and the blood drained from his face as Sinji appeared from the snow as if by magic. An elegant coat of white wolf fur hung from her slender frame and a wave of glistening black hair flowed down the goddess's back. A pair of poison-colored eyes pierced the darkness, glowing with black magic.

"N-no, goddess, I would never think such a thing! I merely say that—"

"You are full of fear," the goddess noted simply. "To show fear is to show weakness. And weakness is something that I will not tolerate in my magnificent army."

"Some of the men seem to have the impression that this mountain is 'haunted,'" Pouja informed her with a low chuckle.

"Yes, as I heard."

Zigmon's mouth fell open. "How—"

"I know everything, Colonel," Sinji snapped. She turned to Pouja. "Shall we begin the search?" Her face showed the innocence of a child.

"I was just about to give the order."

"Then give it, my little king. I want the item. Do whatever you have to do in order to obtain it. Kill anything in your path."

"Surely there will be nothing to kill, my goddess."

"Really? Then what do you suppose killed those Southerners? And don't forget that the prisoner and his captain were not among the dead; I personally checked."

Why did Sinji worry so much about this prisoner? Pouja tapped the side of his helmet as he studied the short woman that stood in the snow, giving off a seductive smile. Surely a single man could not be a match for a god, even if that god was in limbo between the two realms.

"If there is anything in this mountain, my warriors will slay them," Pouja stated bravely.

"Make sure they do. I will not accept failure. I want that item."

Chapter 16
The Next Level

Stuck crawling through the tiny space provided between two rock beds, many of the areas filled with water from the flowing river, claustrophobia began to set into Seramin. All that he could think of was the two gigantic slabs of rock coming together to crush him like a grape. It was definitely not a pleasant thought. With painstaking care the group moved deeper into the mountain, searching for a way out of the deep crevice. None asked why the beasts had not followed them through the entrance of the crevice; they thought it better to believe that the worst danger was behind them now.

After an entire day of crawling downwards, navigating tiny forests of stalactites and stalagmites, and wading through pools of black water, they finally came to the end of the crevice. The torches had gone out long ago and they had been forced to rely on Shoshe's new sight and Aagon's light spells. Seramin still couldn't get over the fact that he was putting so much trust in a girl that a few days ago had no trust in herself. In fact, it seemed that the restoration of her sight had given Shoshe a new spirit. She now began to talk more freely and began smiling.

Running down into the depths of the Ice Maiden the stream of water broke off into many different fingers, but those eventually took a curved path to one entrance in which the inky black water disappeared. It was a doorway, an entrance carved into the rock and guarded by two stone gargoyles. Even this far underground signs of intelligent life could still be found.

The doorway was, in reality, the end of a large water pipe that had been carved inside of the mountain and set so that the water had a way in which to flow. In some places the water was knee deep, but in others it reached up to Hydrib's waist. The water burned with cold, but it was not freezing. That kind of temperature could not penetrate the heavy rock armor of the Ice Maiden, and so the water stayed an unpleasant, but tolerable temperature.

Having drained most of his energy from constantly summoning balls of pure light into his hand to lead the way down the crevice, Aagon set down his pack and broke out the remaining torches. Seramin and Shoshe led the way, carefully moving through the water in order to check for any hidden traps or sinkholes.

"What is this place?" Shoshe breathed, taking in the great craftsmanship that the builders of this temple must have had in order to carve a pipe out of solid rock.

"I don't know; it must be the sub-level of the temple," Aagon answered.

"But why go to all the trouble of building a water pipe?" Hydrib growled, kicking through the deep water.

"Workship's good, good diggers."

"Yes, Greot, you orcs live in the mountains. What good is a water pipe?"

"Water's sometimes inside a mountain, a pipe drains lower levels. Water's sometimes fills them."

"The temple must be down here if the builders went to this much trouble of draining another level of water!" Aagon exclaimed happily.

A splash up ahead stopped the group. The water rippled from something that had fallen in the water.

"What was that?" the priest asked nervously.

"What's do you's see, Shoshe?"

"Nothing, it must have been a rock falling from the ceiling."

"A rock?" Hydrib shook his head and held his torch to the ceiling. "This tunnel is nearly perfect; none of the stone is crumbling."

"Then, what splashed?"

A chattering noise echoed down the pipe, bouncing off of the walls. A rapid series of splashes sounded as the creature swam away.

"Ah, it's just a rat," Aagon said with obvious relief.

"Awfully big rat," Seramin muttered nervously. The Ice Maiden had already revealed the secret of the beast-men in the upper levels; he didn't want another secret to come about.

"If there is a rat down here in the pipe, there must be a dry area nearby."

"I'll lead," Seramin said quickly moving to Shoshe's side.

After several minutes the chattering and squealing of the frantic rat disappeared as the creature distanced itself from the band. The tunnel seemed to stretch on forever, but, finally, there was a light at the end of the tunnel. A light?

"I don't like this, light means something is living down here," Seramin whispered.

"I just hope it isn't any more of those beast things." Aagon gave a shiver.

The pipe broke into a large cavern, even larger than the one that had been blocked off by the wall, but this cavern was even more terrifying.

The water from the pipe weaved through the cavern inside of a deep trench that had been slowly worn down after years of standing up against moving water. Built around the water stood a cluster of shoddy buildings built from every type of scrap wood that Seramin could imagine. They leaned to the side and sagged on rotting foundations. Creaking bridges crossed the river at several points; moss and long trails of mold rolled down, some long enough to brush against the water. All along the bridges and walking alongside the buildings, some of which were as tall as five stories, rats scurried. There were hundreds of them, thousands even. Besides the rats, nothing else moved.

"Could this be the beasts' quarters?"

"Perhaps, but where are they now?" Patting the swords at his sides Seramin reassured himself that they were still in their proper places.

"This not good," the orc whispered. "We's must leave."

"I agree," Shoshe said. She tried to give a smile, but failed and let the fear that she was feeling move onto her face.

That was when they appeared. As silent as shadows small figures dressed in tattered cloaks that dragged against the ground lined the river. In silence they stared down at the intruders of their home. It took a second for any of the members to notice that they had been spotted, and then Shoshe glanced up and gave out a startled squeak.

The others jumped at the sound and drew their weapons, pulling themselves into a tight circle as they quickly swept their gaze over the top of the trench. The figures remained unmoving. Things were not looking good; now hundreds of the cloaked figures lined the river and began filling the bridges.

"What are these things?" Seramin asked Aagon.

"What? Do I look like an expert on these sorts of things? Why is it that everyone thinks that the priests are the smart ones?"

They kept moving, looking for an exit out of the river; weapons raised, waiting for the attack. In the center of the cavern one side of the trench dissolved leaving a slight slope leading to the water's edge. Filling the slope was a crowd of the cloaked figures, these as silent and still as the others. Seramin jumped when several splashes sounded. Some of the figures had jumped into the river, completely encircling them. Summoning what remained of his courage, the captain addressed the creatures.

"I am Seramin of the king's royal soldiers. We mean you no harm!" Maybe with a little persuading the figures would let them go.

"Why do you trespass in our home?" One of the figures standing in the shallows of the river stepped forwards, his dirty black clothes flowing in the current.

"We are looking for a way out of this mountain. Our enemies forced us to flee into the mountain depths."

"Spies you are," the figure accused.

"We are not spies, but we seek your help. We were attacked by—"

"Liars!" the figure hissed. "You are all spies for the Yugarts!"

Yugarts? Was that what the beasts from the surface were called?

"All Yugarts, and their spies must die!" Two tiny hands reached up to the hood of the cloak and pulled it back, revealing the figure's face. Seramin gasped with what he saw.

A rat's head covered in greasy brown fur poked out of the large cloak, two beady red eyes glaring through heavy brows. The creature's snout jutted outwards, and two large pointed teeth peeked out between its lips. These incisors bit and clipped against each other as the red orbs fluttered over the intruders.

"Die you must!" the giant rat snarled. "The Rotters will kill you!"

Out from its cloak the rat pulled a pair of rusted scimitars from their sheaths; they clinked together as he took a fighting stance. The rest of the rats pulled out their own weapons, most being small, hooked blades or daggers like their leader's.

"We don't want to fight you!" Seramin protested as he took a stance of his own.

"A fight you have found, spy of the Yugarts."

In a wave the rats swarmed down into the trench, leaping in and slashing at the band that formed a tight circle around their weakest member, Shoshe.

While the Yugarts focused on sheer strength in fighting the Rotters used cunning and skill with their blades to win the day. Seramin was surprised by their speed and was nearly overwhelmed when two of the rats advanced at his front, blades spinning in front of their faces. Sparks flew as their weapons met Seramin's swords. Turning in a quick circle he cut down both, but three more moved to take their place.

Standing in knee-deep water Aagon used his hammer to squash the rats, who only reached to his chest, like pathetic insects. The heavy weapon would come crashing down on their heads, forcing their broken bodies beneath the water where they would stay. Greot stood like a brick wall, battering a small horde of the creatures with the dull side of his axe. Great swings would send three of the rats flying through the air at a time, but battling with the Yugarts had taught them how to battle this style of fighting and the noose tightened around the orc as the rats moved to cut off and surround him.

Forced into deeper water the prisoner had difficulty wielding his sword and was then forced to use his fists. As the rats swarmed over his body, trying to force him under, he merely plucked them off of his back and smashed in their faces with a mighty blast. Once hit the rat would either swim away with a crushed face, or would slowly sink below the surface in unconsciousness.

Too absorbed with the battle the warriors had been forced away from Shoshe, who now became a sitting duck. Several rats swam their way over to her. Out of the corner of his eye Seramin watched in horror as she floundered in the water, trying her best to escape. Unfortunately, he had other things on his mind, such as the rat leader who was standing before him. The creature had incredible skill with the use of his scimitars and Seramin did everything in his power just to keep out of their reach. The rest of the rats backed away from the two duelers and formed a ring around them, watching in fascination as this enemy matched their leader move for move.

"Die, die, die!" The rat cackled with delight, his evil eyes burning in his head.

"We mean you no harm!" Seramin screamed in rage and frustration as he dodged past a swinging blade, tripping on a spear hidden beneath the water and nearly falling.

"Liar!" the little beast screamed and increased the frenzy of the fight. Their blades became a blur.

The creature then became careless and swung both blades at once towards Seramin's right side. Ducking below the whistling metal the captain thrust low with his sword, preparing to take advantage of the rat's mistake. Then, pain shot through his shoulder as razor-sharp metal sliced through his skin. *What? How?* He pulled away, clutching at his wound.

The rat was smarter than Seramin had expected and the careless attack had really been planned all along. The rat's long pink tail swished behind its back, waving the barbed band attached at the end, giving the creature three weapons instead of two.

"Clever bastard!"

"Thank you."

The situation was getting worse every second.

The rats had drawn closer to Shoshe now. They had pulled the blades from their mouths and began making attempts at slashing at her feet, as she kicked them furiously. Her hand touched the wall. Trapped. "Help!"

The nearest rat stopped swimming and stood upright; water streamed off of its fur and its deadly eyes stared unblinkingly at the girl. The blade in its hand moved as it gave a chuckle. Behind it, seven more rats moved closer.

Before the grinning rat's blade could move to stab Shoshe it gave out a screech and pitched forwards, a hatchet buried deep into its spine. The other rats turned to meet the new threat. Hydrib, bleeding from several cuts from the rats' claws and knives, waded through the water, dragging his sword with a bloody arm. With a mighty throw he hurled the massive blade at the nearest rat. This one managed to duck below the sword, but the rat behind it did not fare so well and became rat on a stick.

Now Hydrib was unarmed, his sword stuck in the impaled rat, and the rest of his wide armament of weapons had already been depleted, embedded in a number of fresh rat corpses. The rats swam towards him now. What threat was this man now that he had no weapons to defend himself? The answer came quickly. He was still a threat. Still as dangerous. Hydrib was always dangerous.

The first rat swung a short sword at Hydrib's head. Unable to move out of the way, he threw his arm into the path of the blade in order to save himself. Clang. The rat's face broke into a frown as its sword bounced off of Hydrib's arm as if it had struck metal; which, in fact, it had.

Out of the sleeves of the prisoner's cloak two long lengths of chain fell into view. An evil grin broke out onto Hydrib's face. The rats began to back away nervously.

The chains twirled through the air, cracking rat skulls and snapping bones in half as if they were dry twigs. Within seconds the five remaining rats were reduced to floating corpses. The killing didn't stop there though. There was still a horde of rats at the landing, and even more crowding along the edges of the trench to watch the bloodshed. Hydrib charged them, armed with the chains.

Blood blossomed with every strike. Crushing skulls with every twist of his arms, Hydrib shouted at the rats, "Come on, come on! Give me a challenge!" Terrified by the savagery of the prisoner the creatures fled, running from the chains that brought so much death to their ranks. Hydrib would have chased them all down and slaughtered them if not for Shoshe's screams to stop.

If she still had her eyes her face would have been streaked with tears. Her breathing ragged and forced, she was near collapse. The rats had already surrendered and the leader had backed away from Seramin, its scimitars lowered, eyeing Hydrib, who was now covered in a fresh coat of splattered rat blood.

"Humph," the prisoner grunted, reluctantly pulling the chains back into his sleeves. His heart pounded painfully against his rib cage, but the blood lust began to reside. Slowly, Seramin turned back to the rat, who quivered like the rodent that it was.

"We did not mean you any harm," he puffed breathlessly.

"Now you will surely kill me now, Yugart scum!" Even facing death the rat managed to show some courage.

"I told you, we aren't spies, we have the same enemy."

"Prove it; all Yugarts are liars."

Seramin slowly put his swords back in their sheaths. Aagon, Greot, and Shoshe sloshed out of the water, shivering and dripping wet as they stood beside the captain and Hydrib. With a wave of his hand Seramin motioned for them to put their weapons away as well.

"See, we are now unarmed, and your life has been spared. Would a Yugart do this?"

"No, I suppose not." The rat looked confused. "If you are not Yugart spies, then what are you?"

"We come from outside of the mountain. I am a human."

"He's a human too?" The creature pointed at Greot.

"No, he's an orc."

"Ah, orcs. We know of them."

"What?" How could this creature not know what a human was, but know about orcs?

"The orcs are the surface dwellers that fought the Yugarts many years ago. Many Yugarts died during that time. The orcs are great warriors."

Seramin gave a questioning look at the priest. Aagon scratched his chin as he thought. "The rat must be talking about the orc invasion of 930."

"But, that was almost two thousand years ago!"

"Have you ever been out of this mountain?" Shoshe asked.

"Yes, long ago, but the gods chose you to be the surface dwellers."

"Surface dwellers?"

"Yes, the chosen ones of the gods, the ones that rule the earth and live under the golden sun."

"Yes, I suppose that would be us."

The cloaked rats looked at each other, excited about the prospect of seeing creatures from the outside world. The leader seemed not to notice his dead comrades that lay at his feet. His tiny paws rubbed eagerly at his cloak. "Come, I must show you the Grey One. We have been waiting for you."

* * * * *

Following Snag Tooth, as the rat was called, through the decaying city Seramin kept one hand on the hilt of a sword as he swept his eyes from left to right. Child-sized rats crowded the sides of the crooked street, pushing at each other so that they could catch a glimpse of the surface dwellers. Waves of normal-sized vermin swept over the ground in masses of rolling brown fur. Shoshe whimpered in fear at the sight of the rats near her feet and pressed up against the captain's back. Aagon prayed silently, his lips moving in wordless hymns to the sun gods.

Mounds of filth lined the streets giving off foul stenches; flies buzzed about in mighty clouds. This, mixed with the smell of unwashed bodies and rotting wood, made Seramin gag, but Greot did not even blink at the stench. Maybe the orcs were immune to terrible smells. For just a moment Seramin became jealous of the green-skin.

Through a twisted mass of towering buildings and crumbling structures Snag Tooth led them. A small army of rat people followed close behind, each armed in some crude manner or another. Daggers, sickles, and rotten spears pointed at the group's back. Moving further into the city Seramin began to lose the feeling of hostility from the rats as the group moved into a bustling market.

Traders sold mushrooms and what appeared to be piles of moss; groups of rats chatted near a crumbling statue of a gigantic rat encased in armor. Rats moved to and fro as if in some kind of hurry, just as the people of Thuringer did. "How-how could this city exist beneath this mountain without us knowing about it?" Aagon asked aloud.

Seramin just shook his head. How many years had these rat people lived in the very center of the Southern kingdom? Where did they come from? At first he thought that the rats could have come from the same origin as the orcs, but they had such a different manner. They were... they were civilized and humanlike. Nowhere did the captain see any of the rats squabble or attack their fellow people. None gave insult to these new intruders, but they did stop and stare in wonder; hushed whispers caught Seramin's ears.

"What are these things?"

"From the surface I heard."

"The prophecies!"

The captain did not have time to ask about the prophecies that one of the rats had mentioned, for they now arrived at a massive shadow that dwarfed the entire city. It took a moment for Seramin's mind to register what he saw.

A giant fortress of solid stone jutted from the southern wall of the cavern. Standing at least seventy feet tall an impregnable wall squatted; an impassible obstacle. Behind the wall a keep peeked out over the barricade like a hermit looking at the men that had knocked on his door, judging the danger, but unwilling to show more of him than was needed.

Now running with excitement Snag Tooth rushed to the bronze gate that guarded the fortress's only entrance. A column of black rats, these larger and more heavily armed than those that Seramin had already seen, stood by the gate. These rats wore old armor that had been polished until the silver had begun to shine from underneath the centuries' worth of filth. Each rat was armed with a heavy halberd, modified to fit their shorter frame. Evil red eyes shone from under closed hoods, regarding the captain and the others with contempt and suspicion.

Looking behind him Seramin noticed that the mob of rats had stopped well short of the wall. Held back by fear they watched from a distance. One of the guard rats, a giant vermin whose armor shone with bronze symbols, listened to Snag Tooth. The rat's eyes grew large and it focused on the group of surface dwellers. Barking an order to the others the rat stepped aside as the gate swung open.

"Follow me," Snag Tooth said with a wave of his paw.

"Where are we going?" Shoshe asked timidly, shrinking away from the intimidating guard rats.

"To see the Grey One. He will want to see the surface dwellers."

"Who exactly is this Grey One?" Hydrib growled without removing his eyes from the black rats, sizing them up.

"Our leader, the most holy one of the Rotters."

"Rotters, is that what your race is called?" the priest asked in surprise.

"Yes, yes, but hurry. We must see the Grey One!"

Moving through the gate to the interior of the wall Seramin noticed that even more rats, much smaller and weaker in appearance than the black guardian rats, manned the walls. Actually, to be more precise, hundreds of rats guarded the walls. The ramparts looked ready to burst as hundreds of dirty brown bodies pushed together for a vantage point overlooking the crumbling city. Armed with spears and crude cutlasses the mob of rats stopped their chattering and fell deathly silent. Seramin felt a shiver travel through his spine as he watched the rats' reactions to their appearance.

Another squad of black rats guarded the entrance to the keep, but once again Snag Tooth talked his way past them. As Snag Tooth disappeared through the doorway Seramin looked at the others who motioned for him to enter first. "Thanks a lot," the captain muttered and ducked through the narrow entrance.

Chapter 17
The Prophecy

Darkness washed through the interior of the keep. Only faint pinpricks of light managed to squeeze in through the tiny windows, but for the most part everything appeared to be a giant shadow. Greot kicked something solid and cursed loudly. The tapping of feet scuttled from side to side as multiple rats moved out of the way of the group.

"Follow me," Snag Tooth called out.

"Where are you, we can't see in the dark!" Seramin answered back.

"I can see," Shoshe whispered with a hidden smile on her face.

"Just follow my voice."

Aagon grumbled, "This is ridiculous." He then summoned the orb of light. Shrieks of pain sounded as the rats shielded their eyes from the burning light.

"Put it out. You are burning our eyes!"

"I will do nothing of the sort. I will not have you stabbing us in the dark."

"We would do nothing of the sort to the surface dwellers." The rat's voice sounded hurt.

"Just the same I would like to see where I am walking."

"Please continue on," Seramin pleaded, motioning for the rat to move. With a small paw shielding his eyes Snag Tooth scampered down the hallway. In the light of Aagon's spell Seramin studied the surroundings. Long tapestries untold centuries old rotted on the walls. Furniture had long since turned to dust and lay strewn about in the various rooms that they passed. Beady red eyes shone in the dark, fearing the light.

Climbing a flight of stairs to the second level the group moved through several more passageways before coming to a long hall lined with tall pillars measuring fourteen feet high. Dark shapes stood between each of the pillars, and Seramin thought they were more of the black rats, but when taking a closer look he stopped in his tracks.

The dark shapes turned out to be suits of armor set so that they appeared to be worn by real people. But something was strange about these suits of armor. They were of excellent design and appeared to be in perfect order while everything else around them seemed to be rotting away. They looked much too heavy for the rats to wear, but they were much smaller than a man, reaching only to Seramin's chest. "Is this what I think it is?"

The group halted and came back to see what Seramin had stopped to look at. Aagon realized what lay before them and his breath caught in his throat. "It is Dwarfish armor," he exclaimed. His hand hovered over the armor as if to touch it, but pulled back, fearful of contaminating the artifact.

"Dwarfs!" Shoshe exclaimed. "I thought they were a myth."

"No, they are very much real. This armor proves it. Look at the runes on the shield." The priest pointed to the strange symbols etched onto the massive slab of metal. "These same runes are found in the El Inu's Esnt'a, the first holy bible of the sun gods. By the sword shall evil be smited. By the shield shall the holy be preserved."

Seramin looked at the armor again as if to assure himself that it was not a mirage. "But if the stories are true the Dwarf race died out thousands of years ago, which would make this armor…"

"Ancient," Aagon finished for him.

"Workship's good," Greot noted with satisfaction.

"I've seen better," Hydrib muttered.

"Do you realize what has happened?" Aagon raced to each suit of armor, glimpsing at the sparkling metal. His voice wavered with excitement. "We are in a Dwarfen fortress!"

"But why now, after all of these years of searching do we finally find one?" Hydrib asked.

"The beast people," Shoshe blurted out.

"The girl is right," Aagon pointed a finger at the girl. "With those beast people guarding the entrance to the Ice Maiden we believed that this mountain was haunted and did not come near."

"We call them Yugarts," Snag Tooth said quietly. Seramin jumped at the sound of the tiny beast's voice, forgetting that the rat had been standing by his side the whole time.

"Yes, I remember you mentioning their name before."

"But there must be more than one Dwarfen fortress in the world. Is it really possible for those...Yugarts to be living in all of them?" Shoshe leaned closer to a suit of armor which hefted a gigantic war axe as she spoke. She blew away a layer of dust and began to cough from the cloud that shot upwards.

"If the Dwarfs were so powerful, why did they vanish?" Seramin questioned aloud.

Aagon spoke up. "The war between the Dwarfs and the Elves must have destroyed their entire race."

"That really doesn't seem possible."

"Not all the Dwarfs left here," Snag Tooth piped up. Everyone paused and turned to the rat.

"What's you's say?" Greot asked cocking his green head to the side.

"You can see some of the Dwarfs if you like."

Aagon leaned over so that his face was mere inches from the Rotter's. "Take us to them," he ordered.

"I would, but only the Grey One can give you permission. You must first talk to him."

"Then show us in."

"Yes, of course. He is just through this door." Pointing to a rotting wooden door at the end of the hallway Snag Tooth guided the group to it. With great care the rat pushed the heavy object open and stepped inside. The room was bare save for a small brazier that burned brightly in the center of the room, outlining a dark figure that sat on the floor. As the group assembled in the room the figure did not move a hair. The flames danced in the dark. Snag Tooth slowly closed the door that thudded with a dull boom.

"Greetings, outsiders." The figure spoke in a dull, creaking voice.

They looked at each other, not knowing what to say. "Are you the one they call the Grey One?" Seramin finally asked.

"Yes, that is what they call me. What, pray tell, are you called?"

"I am Seramin, and my companions are Shoshe, Aagon, Greot, and Hydrib."

"Ah… We have awaited your return, surface dwellers. The prophecy has told of your coming."

"Exactly what did this prophecy say?"

"You do not know of the prophecy? Strange…strange indeed." Surprise filled the Grey One's voice. "I shall tell you our story, but first come and sit." The figure motioned for the group to come closer. Creeping forwards with caution they came until the figure remained sitting only a few feet from them. "Please, sit." The figure leaned closer to the brazier so that Seramin and the others could see its face.

A rat of great age sat before them, its fur grey and back bent like a hunchback's. A tattered, purple robe hung on the rat's withering form, wrapping the creature in a smothering grip. Scars criss-crossed its face, creating a spider web of pink lines. The front teeth had long since rotted from the oracle's mouth, leaving the snout sunken and defenseless looking. The most striking feature of the Grey One were his eyes.

Having long since been ripped from his face the original eyes of the rat had been replaced with two emerald stones set deep into its eye sockets. The stone eyes burned with an intense fire and the rat looked directly at each member of the group, revealing that it was far from blind. A lump caught in the captain's throat when he saw the eyes and he shot a glance at Shoshe, who stared with an open mouth at the strange Grey One.

"I see that my appearance is…unsettling for you," he said.

"Just a little," Hydrib remarked.

"I did not always look this way," the Grey One looked to the side as it began to recall its youth. "I was a young and energetic youth in the past. I loved life and taught myself the ancient languages through the Dwarfen libraries that can still be found in the bowels of this fortress. My life was stolen by the Yugarts. I and several members of my family were captured by the beasts and taken to their lair. There they tortured us and began slaughtering the Rotters one by one until only I remained. The leader took out my eyes, laughing while he cut into my sockets.

"Before the Yugart could complete his act of cruelty the Rotters came to my defense. Killing him, and then carrying me back to the city. There I lost all hope and simply waited for death. I nearly reached that goal; I waited at death's doorstep. But, the gods gave me a vision, a prophecy that one day surface dwellers would come to us. They then led me to the creation of these magical eyes so that I would be able to see once more."

Aagon's mouth twisted into a scowl as the Grey One talked of the gods. "An abomination such as you should not talk of the most holy gods in such a way!" he snarled. Cocking its head to the side the rat looked at the priest.

"And who is this one that addresses me in such a way?"

"I am Aagon, high priest of the sun gods." His chest swelled with pride as he said the words.

"Why do my words offend you, priest? We both speak of the same gods."

"They would not lower themselves to the likes of you. A bunch of rats desecrating the remains of the Dwarfs' home. Just like the orcs, corrupting and destroying."

"We have always lived here, since our creation."

"So you admit your link to the dark gods, Sinji and her evil brother of war?" Aagon began to reach a hand to his war hammer. Seramin noted the rage burning in the priest's eyes and prepared himself to intercept any attack that he launched at the Grey One. The rat might have been an abomination from the underworld, but they still needed to stay on his good graces in order to survive. It seemed doubtful that the tiny group could fight their way through the uncountable thousands of inhabitants in the city.

"The dark gods?" The rat seemed puzzled. "I do not believe that you understand. The gods of the sun created us."

Seramin's heart stopped beating for a second. Shoshe gasped. Even Greot and the prisoner perked up their ears. Sputtering and choking on his words Aagon only managed to croak, "What?"

"The Rotters were created by the gods before their division, but the gods realized their error and banished us to the mountain to spend the rest of our lives."

"Lies! All lies!" Aagon leapt to his feet and began pacing the room, his face flushed with red. "This rat," he pointed an accusing finger at Snag Tooth whom huddled in the corner, "this rat said that there are still Dwarfs in this mountain. I demand to see them! We will see what they have to say about your lies."

The ancient rat spread his arms wide as if to show that he was unarmed before standing. The rat stood a foot taller than Snag Tooth despite the curve in his ancient back. A white tail shaped like a writhing worm slapped against the ground. "You are welcome to see the Dwarfs. But I must tell you that they will not say much."

* * * * *

A column of rats headed by the lurching form of the Grey One moved through the twisting paths of the tunnels that led from the basement of the keep to hidden areas inside the mountain wall. Aagon fallowed close behind, his breathing forced, hands clenching and unclenching at his sides. Ever since talking with the old rat his anger had become a tangible thing.

Seramin knew what bothered the priest, but did not know of a way to calm his nerves. The Grey One had challenged all of the beliefs that Aagon had spent his life believing in. The sun gods were to be the forces of unquestionable truth and wisdom, the creators of only good. The old rat had said that the gods had created the beasts themselves, and what was more, said that the gods had admitted their mistakes.

Aagon now marched on a mission to prove the words of the rat wrong. If he failed, all of his life in the priesthood would be for naught. The Dwarfs would answer his questions, they would set everything right. They were one of the original races; they had been created in the perfect image of Motka.

Walking down the seemingly never-ending passageway Seramin passed the time by looking at the walls. This tunnel had been carved with great care, probably by the Dwarfs themselves. Standing five feet tall and four feet wide the tunnel forced the larger travelers to hunch over. No cracks or seams could be seen in the magnificent workmanship. It appeared that the entire tunnel had been carved out of a solid piece of blue limestone.

Seramin felt his back beginning to hurt from the constant state of walking doubled over, but he did not complain. Hydrib grumbled loudly about the inconvenience, thrice smashing his head against the rock. "When are we gonna get out of this infernal tunnel?" he roared after banging his head once again. Greot tried to muffle his laughter, but caught a lethal glare from the prisoner.

"Almost there," the Grey One rasped, "almost there."

The light from the torches that the rat leader's followers carried moved deeper and deeper into the tunnel until, finally, they stopped. Seramin tried to peek past the bulking form of Aagon to see what they had come to. The sound of a key moving into a lock scraped through the tunnel, and then the rumble of a heavy stone door as it swung aside. "Here is where the Dwarfs lie."

Muscling his way ahead Aagon spilled the rats in all directions. "Where? I don't see anything." Seramin and the rest of the group followed suit, peeking into the wall of black. The Grey One moved deeper into the room, lighting braziers with his torch as he went along. Slowly, the contents of the room became visible.

The ceiling of the room spiraled upwards until even the light of the massive steel braziers could not penetrate the darkness. The walls leapt away from each other, revealing a massive room at least a hundred yards wide and several hundred deep. The grey rat continued to move deeper into the room, lighting braziers as he went; dodging long lines of sarcophaguses as he moved.

There were thousands of the tombs located in the room, each one a large box carved out of stone. Runes circled the sides of the sarcophaguses in a counterclockwise direction. Some of the lids had characters carved into their surfaces, but most remained blank. The Oracle stopped halfway through the giant tomb, leaving untold numbers of sarcophaguses in the unknown.

Aagon walked slowly between two of the rows, hands trailing over the stone as if to prove that his eyes did not betray him. Tears began to swell in his eyes as he began to understand the truth. The Dwarfs had never left the mountain because they had died there. The civilization truly had ended thousands of years ago. His visions of meeting the fabled creatures of the gods vanished in a cloud of dust. All the secrets were dead, lying within the crumbled remains of the Dwarfs inside their stone boxes.

"You see before you the Dwarfs," the Grey One whispered sadly.

"They're all dead," Shoshe stated dumbly.

"Yes." Snag Tooth skittered over to her side. The girl jumped away and the rat withdrew, a hurt look on his voice. "What did you expect?"

"I expected Dwarfs. Living embodiments of Motka. Where are the Dwarfs?" Aagon screamed at the Grey One.

"The Dwarfs are all gone. Dead for centuries."

"How? Did you kill them?" He marched over to Snag Tooth and lifted the tiny creature by the scruff of his neck, shaggy him like a mangy dog. "Answer me!"

"They didn't kill the Dwarfs."

The priest dropped Snag Tooth to the ground and turned to glare at Hydrib. "What did you say?"

"They didn't kill the Dwarfs. Do you really think they would have shown us this crypt if they had? Something else killed them."

"Like who?" Aagon's scream echoed throughout the monstrous cavern. A deep silence answered him, the only kind that can be found in the bowels of a mountain.

"We did not kill them. They were perfect creations," the Grey One protested.

"Then how did they die?" The old rat's guards shrunk away at the sight of the raging priest. Turning his head Seramin realized that Shoshe was nowhere to be seen. She had wandered off somewhere. A pang of fear twisted itself into his gut and the captain grabbed a torch, setting off through the columns of tombs to find Shoshe. The others didn't seem to notice as they listened to the ranting of Aagon.

Seramin's heart began to beat harder in his breast as he moved farther into the cavern. The rows of sarcophaguses seemed to be endless. He began to lose hope of finding the girl and prepared himself to yell her name when a towering shape came into focus. Curiosity overcame Seramin's fears and he crept closer to look at what lay before him.

The tombs ended and a raised podium erupted from the stone floor. A ring of pillars guarded the podium, trailing up into infinity. Climbing the stairs to see the top of the podium Seramin held the torch up to the pillars, trying to make sense of the myriad of runes carved into them. The architecture seemed to be flawless, flowing seamlessly and unblemished even after so many years.

On the podium rested a single sarcophagus, larger and more extravagantly carved than the others. Gold leafing sparkled from the torchlight; the pictures of axes, and age-old battles against the gods of darkness shone in all their glory. At the foot of the gold-encrusted coffin a carving of a Dwarfin warrior wielding an axe and full plate armor knelt in reverence towards Seramin. The creature's long beard brushed the ground, eyes closed in calmness. Beyond the sarcophagus, looking at a stone wall that rose up from the ground, stood the girl. Her hands slightly clenched at her sides, head tilted upwards.

"Shoshe?" Seramin asked cautiously.

"I'm here." The girl sounded dazed, as if she had not really heard what the captain had said.

"What are you doing out here?"

"I found something."

Tossing the torch into a brazier Seramin came to Shoshe's side, waiting for the oil to burn so that he could see what Shoshe's magical vision saw. When the carvings on the wall came into view Seramin began to cry for the others to come.

Chapter 18
History of the Dwarfs

"What is it?" Hydib asked grumpily as he stomped up the steps to the podium.

Seramin stood on the top step, blocking the way as the group assembled at the base. The Grey One, along with his guards, had come as well. The green gemstone eyes glittered in the dark. Seramin stood with his hands crossed, carefully reading the expressions of those that looked at him.

"What did you find?" Aagon grunted, his face still twisted with anger.

"I… I mean Shoshe, found the answer to your riddle."

"You know who killed the Dwarfs?"

"Yes, we know who killed the Dwarfs. It's written on a piece of stone on this platform. It seems that the Dwarfs wanted the truth to be known, even if they all ended up dead. Which, of course, they did."

"Spare us the suspense and let's see this stone," Hydrib growled pushing past the captain, giving a rough shove as he went. Aagon, having once been filled with excitement, slowed to a crawl as he approached the stone. He questioned himself as if he really wanted to proceed with this. Did he really want to know the truth? A feeling in the pit of his stomach told him no, but his mind said yes.

No words appeared on the stone tablet, but rather carvings of small figures that combined to tell the story of the Dwarfs. As the priest decoded the meaning of the tablet he felt his heart sink as he realized the horrible and despicable truth. An acidic taste began to form in his mouth; his gut churned at it felt as if he was about to vomit. Watching the reactions of the priest Seramin translated the tablet for everyone else.

"The Rotters and Yugarts were created back in the time when all four of the gods were still allied with each other. They wanted to create followers, servants. What they created were really slaves. The gods instantly despised what they had made and each broke apart to create their own followers. That was how the Dwarfs came to be. The beasts that had been the gods' first attempts at civilization were used as slaves, forced to build the cities for the 'chosen' ones.

"Then came the great war between the gods of evil and the sun gods. The Rotters and Yugarts were used as cannon fodder by both sides, pushed into battle to soften up the opposing army. They took horrific casualties, reducing their numbers until only a few were left. When the war finally ended the sun gods made one last decision before descending into the third Realm. They attempted to rid the world of anything they considered unclean. Sinji and Kouja were cast into the Realm of the Dead and the beast people were sent to live in exile forever.

"This mountain originally existed to house the beast people. The Dwarfs that lived here were slave herders, using the manpower of their slaves to build everything here, and made sure that nothing escaped. But, the Yugarts didn't like their new masters. A civil war erupted. The Yugarts rose up and killed the Dwarfs one by one. It was a slaughter. They had nowhere to go. The Rotters, according to this carving, fought with the Dwarfs, but they could not stand against the Yugarts. The Yugarts escaped to the surface while the rats stayed down here. The Rotters didn't kill the Dwarfs. The beasts on the surface did."

Seramin watched as Aagon's legs began to quiver. Unable to stand under his own power the priest backed away from the tablet as if it had become a monster ready to consume him. Bumping into the massive sarcophagus he sat down. Great teardrops streamed down his face. "I can't believe it."

"You better believe it, priest," Hydrib gloated. "Your gods aren't the perfect beings that you had made them out to be."

"Shut your mouth, you—you heretic!"

"Heretic? Is that what you call those that tell you the truth?" The prisoner jabbed a finger at the tablet. "Look for yourself! Everything is right there!" Aagon refused to look. The figures carved in the stone now stood only to mock him. Seramin felt a twang of pity for the priest. Everything that he had lived for had been for nothing. His prayers, his actions, even the wars he had fought had been for naught.

"We are abominations of the earth," the Grey One said sadly. "The gods made a mistake by placing us here."

"There must be some good in you," Shoshe comforted.

The ancient rat shook his head sadly. "No, young child. Our only purpose now is to guard the sacred object that the gods have hidden here. That is all that is left in our life."

Everyone turned to stare at the rat, even Aagon stopped his weeping to look up. "What object?" Hydrib asked, his words dripping with purpose.

"Why, a sacred object in the lowest level of the mountain. We were never told what it was exactly, but we were told to let no one take it."

"But it isn't on the tablet," Seramin protested, pointing at his evidence.

"Baw, it was never spoken of." The Grey One waved a hand dismissively. "The Dwarfs did not want it found; they thought that if they did not speak of it no one would learn of its presence."

"But's why's do you's tell us?"

"You are not the only ones that have enemies. We and the Yugarts have been at war for centuries and we thought…" The old rat trailed off and Snag Tooth picked up for the Grey One.

"We know where the object is kept, but we cannot open the door into the chamber. We thought that maybe if you could retrieve the object then you could use it to defeat the Yugarts. I have never seen the sun. We all want to escape this accursed mountain."

"Trust me; it ain't much better on the outside." Hydrib laughed.

"Please, would you do this?" the Grey One pleaded. "We would always be in your debt."

Seramin shook his head. "I don't know. I don't have a good feeling about this."

Leaping from the ground Aagon grabbed the captain by the arm and dragged him away from the rest of the group. When they were at a great enough distance to keep their conversation secret the priest released his grip.

"Do you not realize the opportunity that has been granted to us?" he hissed.

"We don't know anything about this magical object."

"Exactly, who knows how powerful it could be! Perhaps it would aid us in our defeat of the North."

"Yes, but..." Seramin's mind was beginning to swim with thoughts. "There must have been a reason for the sun gods to hide it in this mountain. Something isn't right."

"Are you crazy? Think of the lives that could be saved. Think of the kingdom, or your family..." Aagon didn't know it, but he had struck the magical chord with Seramin. The captain looked over to Shoshe, poor blind Shoshe that looked so much like his own daughter. If he had this fabled item could he have prevented her blindness? But why did Aagon want this item? Was it some sort of way to rationalize what he had learned abut the gods? Did he have his own intentions for the object?

"Fine. We'll go get the item."

Aagon beamed and slapped Seramin on the back. The captain did not know why the learning of this item's presence had so suddenly changed the priest's mood, and it did not thrill him to see the priest this way. Returning to the Grey One Seramin agreed to the rat's request.

"We'll get the item for you, rat. Just show us the way."

"Excellent. I wish that I could join you, but Snag Tooth will have to do. You see... I am needed at the city." He gave a weak smile. "I have just received word that we are being attacked."

Chapter 19
The Sword of Ice

"You know of these black warriors?" Snag Tooth asked nervously as he scurried down a dark tunnel, leading the group to the bottom of the mountain where the item lay in wait. He was referring to the mysterious humans dressed in heavy armor that had emerged into the Rotter's home.

"Yes," Seramin admitted, "they are our enemy. They must have followed us into the mountain."

"But, they's fight with's the Yugarts?" Greot puzzled.

The runner shook his tiny rat head. "No, the black warriors are fighting against the Yugarts, but the enemy is following them as they move towards us. The Grey One has ordered that the people move into the tunnels to swarm the enemy as they draw near, but there are so many of them."

"We will help you," Seramin offered, but the rat shook its head.

"No, the Grey One says that you must find the item. It is the will of the gods that the evil ones do not get it, so it is up to you to find the source of power before…they do." Then to himself, "I cannot leave my people," Snag Tooth whispered, pounding himself on the head, hating himself for leaving those that he cared about defenseless.

"But you need to show us the way, or we won't find the item," Shoshe piped up.

"Yes, but I still hate it."

"Will you's win?" Greot asked while looking down at the tiny Snag Tooth.

The rat sadly shook his head. "I think not. Our numbers are too weak right now. Our main weapon against the Yugarts was that they didn't know where our home is. But, with them moving down the northern tunnel they will come right to the village. It will be a slaughter. The troops can only buy us time."

"We must hurry then, let their sacrifice be not in vain." The priest gave a quick prayer to the gods. Whether it be for himself or the rat people no one could tell.

With the rat leading the way they ran through a small side tunnel that quickly turned into a swirling staircase that spiraled downwards. The steps had been cut carefully, and even a small stone railing had been carved into the wall. The staircase seemed to go on forever, until it finally split off and continued straight down a long and narrow tunnel. As he ran Seramin felt the air grow noticeably colder, soon his breath was turning to frost and he began to shiver.

The sounds of battle followed the group as they distanced themselves from the city. Swords clashed together and the squeals of pain vibrated down into the Ice Maiden's depths. Roars of rage from the Yugarts shook the very walls while the vile prayers of the Northerners continued throughout the bloody battle.

The hallway suddenly ended, plugged by a stone door identical to the one that lay broken a mile above their heads.

"This it?" Greot puffed. His head nearly disappeared from the frozen air crystals that surrounded him and he had to stoop over to avoid hitting his head against the ceiling.

"Yes, the item is in there, untouched or seen for centuries."

"But how do we get through the door?" Seramin wailed.

"Leave that to me." The priest rolled up the sleeves of his shirt and hefted his hammer. "You might want to step back."

Muttering a spell Aagon held his hammer high, waiting until the stone head glittered with blue light, and then he struck the door's surface. The stone shuddered, and a great booming noise echoed through the tunnel, but it stayed in place. Banging against the door again and again Aaron worked until the door's protective spell couldn't stand up to the punishment anymore and the stubborn stone flew from its hinges, sliding away with a loud grating noise.

Slowly, carefully, they moved into the small chamber; Seramin took the lead.

A blast of frigid air swirled around in the chamber, being cold enough to cause the captain's eyes to burn. The room was filled with snow and ice; the walls bordered with stone statues of knights in armor, each one covered in a coat of ice crystals. In the far corner water had somehow leaked into the chamber centuries ago and had frozen solid.

In the center of the chamber stood a podium of grey stone. No ice touched this podium, but in its center sat something that shined like silver.

The sword was long, reaching five feet in length and created out of a silver metal that gleamed in the snowy room. On each side of the handle a gaping skull screamed in silence; two similar, yet larger skulls bulged from the bottom of the blade. Each mouth spewed forth a steady stream of freezing mist that pooled on the floor. Air currents sent the mist swirling to form a vortex around the podium.

"This—what is this?" Seramin stammered.

"This is the item," Aagon said softly, examining the sword from a distance. "I can feel the energy from here."

True enough Seramin felt a slight vibration in the air as if the sword hummed with the excitement of the release from its prison.

Roars echoed down the hallway into the chamber as the Northerners pushed farther into the mountain, battling the Yugarts and the Rotters all the way. They would reach the chamber in only a few seconds. There was no time to contemplate any longer; it was time to make a stand and fight.

"Shoshe, go hide!"

"But…"

"Do it! They're coming."

Like a wave crashing into the shore the enemy charged through the doorway. Dressed in black cloth and silver armor the Northerners came with swords swinging and axes chopping. Close behind came a wave of Yugarts, their animal feet carrying them swiftly across the stone. Seramin knocked a sword aside then skewered the owner, quickly retracting the blade so that he could twist to his side and stab a nearby beast in the chest.

The battle was a crazy three-on-three battle royal with Seramin and his companions caught up in the middle and fighting for their very lives. There was no time to catch one's breath, or to back away and allow the fighting to take its course and make the two enemy forces to weaken each other. The air filled with the sounds of slashing blades and blood as it squirted from severed arteries.

Snag Tooth rolled about the ground, spinning and leaping with the look of an acrobat, scimitars cutting into flesh. Greot chopped down Yugarts as if they were saplings, and the priest swung his hammer from side to side with devastating effect. The only one that Seramin couldn't see was Hydrib, the prisoner.

The feeling came at first as a slight tingling in his neck, followed by a burning as if fire had crept underneath the collar like a living thing and had begun burrowing into Seramin's neck. Smoke shot out in streams from the intense heat. The pain became so intense that the captain was almost decapitated by an axe that he barely managed to block. Then, visions began to flash through his eyes as if they were his own, memories that he was starting to remember now, but these were someone else's memories.

Some unknown battlefield littered with dead bodies, the wounded screaming in silent cries of anguish. Thuringer, wrapped in flames as thousands of burning arrows flew over the walls in the smoke-filled night. A trio of bodies swaying slowly from side to side, attached to a tree limb with rope around their necks; a woman and two children. Seramin couldn't see their faces, the sun was behind them and their bodies were blackened.

Hydrib let out a scream from behind Seramin as he raised his sword, preparing to crush the captain underneath with the weapon's massive size. His face was a mask of pure rage, lips peeled away from white teeth. Now would be the time that he broke free from his captor.

Leaping to the side the captain threw himself to the ground as the sword slammed into the stone tiles, cracking the floor. Before he could rise to his feet Seramin was slammed backwards as he caught a glancing blow on the chin from the side of Hydrib's boot. Stars leapt into his eyes as his limp body slid a cross the ice. Loose fingers opened up and the captain's weapons slid away from him in the confusion of the battle.

It would have been over right then and there if it was not for the flock of Northerners and Yugarts that unknowingly jumped between the captain and the prisoner. Hydrib punched a Northerner with one hand and sliced a Yugart neatly in half, then set to the task of clearing the living obstructions that had come between him and his freedom.

Shaking his head Seramin tried to clear the cobwebs. He felt blood running down his face, and his jaw had become stiff. Climbing shakily to his feet the captain looked around dumbly for his swords, but, of course, they were nowhere to be found among the rush of feet and piles of bodies. Standing there, shining in the white light, was the silver sword that sat frozen in the stone pillar. Mocking him, calling him closer it seemed. Stumbling to the weapon, Seramin grabbed the cold handle and gave a mighty pull.

It came out with surprising ease, sliding out of the stone as if coming from a scabbard, ready for battle. The skulls stared unblinkingly at him; they thirsted for blood, and they would quickly get their fill in the already blood-soaked room.

A Northerner charged at Seramin, who took a defensive position, waiting until the man came close enough to strike. Parrying the barbarian's attack the captain lopped off his arm, which went spinning to the floor. The wounded warrior stared at his stump in wonder, for it did not bleed. The blood had begun to spurt out, but then it had frozen instantly creating a red spike that jutted from his arm. The severed hand was also frozen solid, the sword still locked in an iron grip.

Another warrior came by, and Seramin cut into his stomach with similar results; blood spray turned into red ice shrapnel, and the wounded man shriveled up as his intestines turned to ice. *What sort of sword is this?*

Hydrib had now muscled his way through the blockade leaving a mound of corpses behind and came bearing down on Seramin. He had seen what the sword had done to the two unlucky men that it had cut, but he seemed neither surprised nor afraid of the magical weapon. The two swords met with a mighty clang that rang out above the din of the battle. Weapons crashing in the air, each opponent cringed as the burning in their necks intensified; they could feel their skin shrivel and scorch. Neither stood down. The two blades met again near the podium as Seramin blocked a chopping attack by the prisoner and they held their swords together, trying to force the other to back down with pure strength.

"Give up, Seramin. You are no match for me."

"And you are no match for this sword," Seramin spat back, the mist from the sword pooled over Hydrib's sword, covering it with ice crystals.

An evil light gleamed in the back of Hydrib's eyes. "Oh, really? You're not the only one that can play with fire!"

The prisoner's sword burst into flame, tongues red-orange flicked out into the air. The intense heat started Seramin's clothes to smolder, but the sword in his hands remained as cold as ice, the flames didn't even affect the powerful magic that surrounded it. Hydrib pushed the captain backwards off of the pillar where his feet caught nothing but air and he fell to his back. As quick as lightning he jumped back to his feet and blocked the burning sword, quickly giving ground to the living fury that stood before him.

Aagon could not believe his eyes; Seramin was now locked in battle with the prisoner, the one who was supposed to obey the every command of the captain; what's more, the prisoner's sword now blazed, wreathed in flame, burning any unlucky foe that drew too close to the two duelers into charcoal. Most of the Northerners and Yugarts had by now been disposed of and it became apparent that Seramin needed help. Hydrib intercepted the priest with surprising ease and turned to the defensive, using the burning sword as an impassible wall.

"Do you think your little friends can help you now, Seramin?" he taunted despite the pain he felt from the collar.

"You may be strong, but together we will defeat you!"

"Ha! I don't know how to fail!" With that Hydrib stopped his retreat and lashed out at Seramin, catching the captain off guard with the sudden change in direction.

Throwing the silver sword in front of him in desperation the captain closed his eyes and waited for the inevitable biting of the flames against his skin. But, they never came. The skulls spewed out a great cloud of mist that caught the sword in midswing, along with the side of Hydrib's face. Howling in a combination of rage and fear the prisoner looked down with a cracked and bleeding face.

The flames themselves had frozen to the sword, giving it a spiked and reptilian look. The fire had gone out and the black sword had returned to its original dull appearance. Aagon saw this chance to attack, but Hydrib would not be stopped now. His free hand snatched the hammer out of the air with a thump. The priest's eyes grew wide with surprise as the flat side of the ice-covered sword connected with his stomach. He flew backwards, smacking his head against a statue.

Swinging around, fire now burning in his eyes, Hydrib knocked the magical sword from Seramin's hands with one swing. Unarmed the captain backpedaled in desperation. When his feet came in contact with the ice he lurched backwards as it crackled under his feet; it was not completely frozen after all. He was trapped; Hydrib stood in front of him and the half-frozen water blocked his exit.

There was only one thing he could do.

When Hydrib swung to decapitate Seramin he ducked low, pulled a dagger from his boot, and jammed it deep into the prisoner's ribs. Giving a mighty bellow Hydrib grabbed Seramin's collar with a massive fist, lifted him above his head, and threw him down against the ice with all of his awesome strength. The ice wasn't strong enough to stand up to so much force and the captain's body disappeared from view, icy water bubbling up from the hole.

The coldness pierced his lungs, the freezing water attacking his skin like millions of tiny needles that jabbed at once. Seramin's first impulse was to take a breath, but he somehow managed to hold the tiny amount of precious air in his lungs. The world under the ice appeared surprisingly bright, as if some large spotlight had been put on the surface and beamed through. The light illuminated a collection of skeletons, all of them Dwarfs, lying down in a watery grave that stood only three feet deep. Weapons of every kind—maces, spears, swords, clubs, axes, and halberds—were scattered among bits and pieces of rusted armor and shredded clothing.

Climbing onto the sagging ice, water bubbling around his feet, Hydrib began to chop downwards, trying to pierce the fine white crystal that Seramin had become trapped beneath. Water and ice chips sprayed in the air as the prisoner pounded in a fury.

"Where are you, you bastard?" he raged. "Come out and fight like a man! I've waited too long for you to ruin this for me!"

The ice above Seramin began to crack and splinter, the blade of the black sword burst through, traveling down to the floor where it thudded dully; the sword repeatedly burst through the ice, slowly working its way towards the captain in a zigzagged path. In the far corner of the ice-covered prison rested a long spear with a point sharp enough to pierce through the ice, but it was a long way off with Seramin's lungs beginning to burn.

Crawling through the skeletons and rusted shards of metal that cut and scraped his skin, the captain reached for the spear, his fingertips barely brushing the handle.

WHOOMP!

The black sword burst through the ice, barely missing his left leg.

WHOOMP!

This time it missed his right shoulder by a bare inch.

"Why won't you just die? Why won't you roll over like a dog? Why won't—" Hydrib's words were cut short when a rusted spearhead burst through the ice and struck his stomach, cutting deep into the soft tissue. He doubled over, clutching at the weapon that had impaled him. Under the ice Seramin watched as a dark puddle began to grow on the ice.

With one more burst of strength Hydrib gripped the handle of his sword in both hands and drove it through the ice one last time. The weapon shook as it struck its target and the waters below him turned red.

"No!" Shoshe screamed in terror from her hiding place behind one of the statues. Her hand covered her mouth as if it alone held back her fear. Seramin was dead, Hydrib had killed him! The prisoner slowly turned his head to eye Shoshe; his eyes cold and unforgiving. Turning away from the blind girl Hydrib pulled his sword from the ice, and the spear from his stomach, and began to lurch towards Aagon, who was now beginning to rise from the ground, clutching at a tender stomach.

Now all of the enemies had been eliminated, all but one, the prisoner who had never really been a friend at all. Greot the orc, and Snag Tooth the rat-like Rotter jumped out in front of their comrade, weapons raised and prepared to sacrifice their lives for him. Unfortunately, Hydrib still remained strong enough to swat them both aside with relative ease. Having been given enough time to find his war hammer and rise back up onto shaky legs, Aaron met Hydrib once again.

The prisoner's attacks were now somewhat weaker from the wounds that he had received, but Aagon had not fully recovered from the blow he had received and his hammer waggled in the air. His face strained as he met the prisoner's attacks.

"Give up, old man, it's over!"

"Never!"

"You're weak!"

"I'm still stronger than you think I am!"

"Prove it," Hydrib growled, attacking with all of the strength he could muster with the near-mortal wound to his belly. Falling back from the relentless offensive Aagon fell to a knee. Holding the hammer above his head the priest felt his grip weaken as one shattering blow after another fell upon his weapon. The force of the blows caused his arms to grow numb and he felt the strength draining from his body.

Bursting out of the ice Seramin stumbled; one hand clutched the spurting wound on his side while the other gripped the spear. Raising the spear he hurled the weapon with all his remaining strength. He then collapsed onto the ground, but his aim proved to be true.

The spear dug deep into Hydrib's back. Lurching backwards the large man locked up due to the freezing pain, his back arched and chest extended outwards. Aagon didn't wait, his hammer crashed into the prisoner's chest, crushing ribs and throwing him down to the ground. The prisoner did not get up again.

"Seramin!" Shoshe cried as he raced to the wounded man's aid. She immediately began ripping pieces of cloth from her clothes to bind his wound and began a healing spell. It hurt badly, but Seramin would live. He had suffered far worse and the girl had seen him through it.

"Hydrib had's magic sword?" Greot asked curiously as he limped over, trying to use Snag Tooth, who barely reached past his waist, as a support.

"Yes, it appears so."

"I knew he was evil," Aagon said bitterly, casting a glare at the prisoner's crumpled body.

"Yes, but unfortunately neither of us was able to see that he would turn on us."

Snag Tooth's head darted from side to side during the conversation; his acute ears picked up the sounds of more Yugarts as they drew closer. The battle was not over yet.

"The enemy is drawing near, we must leave."

Seramin nodded his head. "Right, but not without the sword."

The girl ran over to where the magical sword lay and brought it back to Seramin. "It's cold," she remarked.

"Yes." Seramin took it in his hand and the coldness that was creeping into his body from the water vanished. A feeling of warmth spread from his sword hand and through the rest of his body.

"There is powerful magic in that sword," the priest noted, "just as in Hydrib's, but perhaps this magic is for good."

"I sure hope so, because it's gonna take a miracle to escape from this mountain."

"I can lead you out. We Rotters know of hundreds of passageways that the Yugarts know nothing about," the rat piped up.

"I hope you're right, I don't think I can make it through another fight."

* * * * *

After Snag Tooth led Greot and the three humans towards the surface a pack of Yugarts shambled into the chamber, taking in the piles of dead that lay strewn about. The leader, a strong-looking beast with curving horns covered in ornamental trinkets, sniffed the air; the smell of death was overpowering in the tiny space.

In the center of the floor a single figure stirred. A large man dressed in black with a spear protruding from his back reached out for a sword that remained only inches from his outstretched hand. Dirty fingernails scratched at the handle. Blood pooled from his wounds, and each breath was labored from the broken ribs, but he still refused to give up. He had waited for too long to fail, he did not know how to fail.

Hefting its axe the Yugart leader swaggered across the room, stopping so that it remained standing over the mortally wounded man. Hydrib's eyes turned upwards just as the axe began its descent.

Chapter 20
Escape

Sinji reveled in the bloodshed as she stood among the rat city, inhaling deeply in order to catch the scent of burning flesh. The city sizzled as the slaughter of the inhabitants commenced. Hundreds of Northern warriors worked their way forward against the endless waves of rat people that threw themselves relentlessly at the invaders. Pouja's personally handpicked warriors easily chopped the abominations to death. The streets ran red as rivers of blood poured into the gutters.

Pouja stood by the goddess's side, waiting for further orders. His armor was splashed with red gore. One hand clenched the handle of his sword which dripped with crimson. The Northerners had entered the mountain, many of the men worried about ghosts and daemons. But, their fears vanished when the Yugarts attacked. Years of warfare had dimmed their feelings to bloodshed, and seeing a killable enemy brought about a blood lust that none could control. They methodically worked their way to the bottom of the mountain, killing as they went. Reaching the rat city the men had thrown themselves at the rats, at first not realizing the colossal odds that lay stacked against them.

Although greatly outnumbered, the warriors refused to be pushed back by the living wave. The tide turned with the return of the Yugarts. Pouring out from the side tunnels they refocused their attack on their lifelong enemy, the Rotters. Now being attacked on three sides, the rats were pressed in and growing frantic. Losing all sense of tactics they threw their lives away in futile attacks.

"Push forwards!" Zigmon cried, rallying those around him with a wave of his axe. The colonel had thrown himself totally into the fray, trying to strengthen his image in the dark goddess's eyes. He wanted to show here that he did not question her rule, and he would not show weakness.

Buildings blazed, the rotting foundations bursting into flames as the attackers threw torches against the wood. Given the choice of burning alive or facing the blades of the Northerners the Rotters were continually moving in and out of the entrances as the flames grew taller. They raced out to escape the growing heat, but the veteran warriors pushed them backwards time and time again. The air inside the cavern began to grow heavy with smoke, making breathing difficult.

The atmosphere reminded Sinji of home. Hell had come to the Ice Maiden, and soon only death would remain. Reaching out with a slender hand the goddess patted Pouja on the shoulder. The king spun around, his surprised expression hidden behind his helm.

"Make sure you leave some of the creatures alive, my king. I have something special planed for them."

"Yes, goddess."

"Once this city, and the fortress fall, we will be able to search for the item."

Rats made a mad dash for the gates of the fortress, but the walls were already stuffed full of bodies. Those outside the walls pounded their tiny fists against the bars and begged for help. But those that had managed to reach safety could only watch as the enemy cut them down one by one. Grabbing old beams that had once served to support houses the warriors began to batter at the gates. The old metal slowly began to warp and crack under the pressure. The fortress had only bought time for the Rotters.

Sinji cackled with glee. A red light leapt from her fingertips as a spell blasted a group of rats from the walls. The item would be hers. And then, hell would come to the rest of this miserable world. Literally.

* * * * *

"My home!" Snag Tooth screeched as he emerged into the cavern. He fell to his knees and began to weep as he saw the carnage before him. The others stopped by the rat's side. Seramin laid a hand on the furry creature's shoulder; Shoshe whimpered in fear.

"They never stood a chance," Aagon said grimly.

"They're killing my family. They're dying!" Snag Tooth threw his hands up in despair. All that he loved was now destroyed, being consumed by flames.

Most of the city was now ablaze; even from the distance from where they stood the group could see piles of slain rats. A ring of Northerners stood by the fortress gate, cheering on a group of twenty or so men as they pounded relentlessly at the gates. When the ancient metal finally gave way with a terrifying screech the black wave surged inside. A woman stood in the center of the Northerners; spells flew from her fingertips in a flurry of colors. Rats screamed and died under the barrage of magical energies. Great chunks of wall fell to the ground and holes were ripped into the ranks of rats with each explosion.

"If we stay here any longer the Northerners are going to find us," Aagon noted with a touch of fear in his voice.

"Snag Tooth," Seramin grabbed the rat's shoulders and spun the creature around so that he looked into the Rotter's eyes, "do you know a way out?"

"I-I don't know…"

"We's need's to now!" Greot nearly shouted.

"If we stay here we'll die. We need you to remember a way to the surface."

"I-I think I know of a way. But, the Yugarts guard it."

"They's is all down's here," the orc noted.

"Just show us the way. We'll worry about the Yugarts later." The captain hauled the crying Snag Tooth to his feet and shook the poor rat until his head snapped back and forth. "Stay with me," he ordered.

"But…I…" Snag Tooth blubbered, the fur by his eyes moist with tears.

"Hey! Life's tough, get over it." Seramin screamed into the rat's face. "This is your chance for freedom. Show us the way to the surface."

As Snag Tooth led the band into one of the cavern's numerous side tunnels a barbarian watched their movements. Zigmon wiped a blob of gore from his chin as he considered what to do. He could tell the king about the group that had just disappeared. But, why should he get all the glory? If he could capture the human captain all by himself the goddess would surely reward him. No one else would notice his absence. The chaos of the battle would surely rage onwards for several more hours as the last of the defenders were mopped up.

* * * * *

Having regained his composure Snag Tooth led the way through the dark tunnel as Aagon lighted the way with his spell. Everything became a blur to Seramin as the group moved in a direction that more or less took them away from the fighting. They passed great caverns that held large lakes of crystal-clear water. Rooms full of stalactites and stalagmites created confusing mazes that needed to be navigated. They raced up what seemed to be never-ending staircases that the Dwarfs had carved into the mountain so that they could mine the veins of ore.

Suddenly jerking to a halt Snag Tooth turned to look at the others. "Where...now?" Shoshe panted heavily. The rat looked as if he had barely run and his breath had hardly increased. Even Greot the orc was winded. A crooked finger pointed to a mound of rubble piled against the wall.

"Through there."

"Through where?" Aagon nearly shouted.

"There's a door on the other side of these stones. We piled them here so that the Yugarts could not enter."

"That's going to take us forever!" Shoshe protested.

"It's that or go back through the city..." Snag Tooth trailed off. The others looked at each other for a moment before attacking the stones.

Seramin strained to lift the heavy rocks. He had no clue how the tiny rats had accomplished this feat and gritted his teeth as he felt his spine bend under the colossal weight. Slowly, yet surely, the pile diminished. Soon half of the doorway could be seen; an old steel object badly stained and rusted with age, yet still solid. But, that was when they heard the noises.

"What that?" Greot asked, suddenly dropping the stone he had been carrying and nearly crushing Aagon's foot underneath.

"Watch it, you—"

"Quiet!" Seramin hissed. "I heard it too."

The others strained their ears to catch what noise the orc and the captain had picked up. The stomping of feet and the soft ting of metal against stone vibrated through the cave.

"It's the Northerners. They're coming!" Shoshe squealed in terror.

"Quick, get the door open!"

Clawing at the stones they desperately tried to free the door of the last of the rubble. Pulling the final stone away Seramin grabbed the handle and gave it a mighty twist.

It remained stuck.

"Stand back!" Moving into position Aagon hefted his hammer and began smashing against the metal.

Sweat began to pour from the priest's face as he tried to force the door open. The battle with Hydrib and the mile or so he had just ran had drained the last of his energy, and it took all of his strength just to swing his hammer. Summoning another spell was out of the question. He feared that the willpower required would cause him to faint. Slowly, agonizingly, the door began to peel back like melting wax. Soon a hole large enough even for Greot to squeeze through had been pounded in.

"Quick, I can see the light from the torches!" Seramin whispered frantically, as if the Northerners hadn't heard the noise that Aagon had just caused.

Groaning with fatigue the priest jumped through the hole into the blackness. Shoshe was next, soon followed by Snag Tooth, Seramin, and finally Greot, who with much grunting and groaning managed to squeeze his massive bulk through.

"Aagon, can you cast your illumination spell?" the captain asked quietly.

"I don't think so, I have no energy left." The priest's words felt hollow; even they had been stripped of their energy.

"I can show you the way." Shoshe offered grabbing the captain's hand. "Which way, Snag Tooth?"

"Go left, the ground slopes upwards," the rat answered before setting off to lead the group.

Seramin felt totally defenseless without being able to see where he was going. Being led by the girl he tensed his muscles as if waiting for something to jump out and grab him. And, due to the fact that the Northerners were chasing them the group had to hurry. The captain just knew that he was going to run into a wall. That was why he was so surprised when his foot caught something and he was sent sprawling onto the ground.

"What the hell?" he sputtered.

"You tripped over the tracks," Shoshe explained while stooping low to help him up.

"The what?"

"There's a pair of tracks on the ground. The dwarfs must have used this tunnel to cart away dirt and rocks and stuff."

"Where's does this tunnel's go's?"

"Well, I-I don't actually know."

"What!" Seramin would have slapped the rat upside the head if he could have seen the creature.

"I've never been here before," the rat said quickly in defense. "This was territory belonging to the Yugarts."

"Then how do you know where we're going?"

"Tunnel's goes up. Will's go to surface."

"Are you sure about that, orc?"

"I's live's in a cave."

Seramin's side began to cramp up, but he continued pushing forwards, one hand holding onto Shoshe's while the other reached out to intercept any obstacles that decided to jump into his path. The Northerners were drawing closer. Shouts rang out as they sensed that they were drawing closer to their prey. A few more minutes and everything would be over. Then, a tiny ray of silver light appeared at the end of the tunnel.

The captain couldn't believe his eyes at first. But, as he continued to run, the light grew steadily brighter. Aagon whooped for joy and Shoshe gave a shout as they saw the light too. Soon Seramin could see his surroundings and did not need to hold on to Shoshe's hand.

A set of iron tracks ran the length of the tunnel. On them a collection of metal carts, some still full of dirt and rocks, sat ready to be dumped or refilled. A few picks and shovels even lay on the ground. Seramin would have liked to pick them up and hold the objects in his hands. But the pursuers forced the group to continue moving.

His chest heaved; the air became difficult to breathe. It seemed that they would never reach the end of the tunnel, but they somehow managed to continue moving. Not one member of the group wanted to die in the gods' forsaken mountain. They all had something to live for. A small Dwarfen doorway stood ajar, revealing an area full of silver light. Quickly ushering the others through Seramin slammed the metal vault behind him, locking out the barbarians.

The shaft was shaped like a massive, vertical stone cylinder. Measuring sixty feet in diameter it spiraled up for hundreds of feet, reaching for the top of the mountain. A wide assortment of wooden ladders, scaffolding, and crumbling bridges led the way to the surface. At regular intervals doors identical to the one that Seramin had just slammed shut led to different levels in the mountain. All were shut tight and rusted. Chains connected to pulley systems dangled from the walls, hanging like metal vines.

The group now stood on a wooden platform that overlooked the half-finished construction. Granting himself the courage to look down Seramin felt his brain spin as the cylinder continued downwards into oblivion. Grabbing hold of the railing he pulled himself away from the never-ending fall.

"What do we do now?" Aagon wailed as he looked at the gigantic puzzle that now blocked their way.

"I guess we climb." Shoshe shrugged her shoulders.

"This wood is thousands of years old. Do you really think it's going to hold our weight?"

"Everything's worked so far's." Greot gingerly tested the weight of the platform with his feet by bouncing up and down.

"The Yugarts have used this as a passageway to reach the lower levels of the mountain in their raids. It will hold," Snag Tooth assured.

The door shook with an audible boom as something solid struck it from the other side. The Northerners were forcing their way through! "It looks like we don't have a choice." Seramin pushed the others towards the nearest ladder. "We climb." Double-checking to make sure the silver sword still remained strapped to his back the captain began to scale the cylinder-shaped shaft.

The climb proved to be even more difficult than he had originally imagined as the climb changed from ladders, to scaffolding, to shimmying up chains, and back to ladders every few feet. The ancient pins that held the rotting contraptions together groaned in protest with each movement. Wooden beams crackled and snapped underfoot. Each person took their different route upwards, distancing themselves from the others as they decided that their path was the best choice.

The battering against the door ended as the hinges snapped under the relentless pounding. Pouring into the room the Northerners looked about in amazement at the oddity of the Dwarfen digging. Then, seeing Seramin and the rest as they frantically climbed towards the surface, the leader pointed up and ordered his men to pursue. Too tired from earlier events Seramin knew that they had no chance of outclimbing the men and pulled out the magical sword in preparation for battle.

The first Northerner met Seramin halfway up a ladder and thrust out with a sword, barely missing the captain's legs. Kicking out Seramin pushed the blade away and scurried higher up to get away from the man that so intended to kill him. More warriors followed the other, adding more weight than the ladder could take.

"Stop, you're going to break it!" the captain shouted at the warriors, but they did not pay attention to his warnings, and soon the metal pins that had held the ladder to the stone wall for so long popped out one by one. Seramin hooked his arms through the rungs as the wooden ladder began to tip forwards over the cavern.

His scream caught in his throat as the captain felt himself become weightless. Pitching forwards the ladder struck the opposite side of the wall, snapping at the point of impact. Continuing to fall the ladder jammed tightly once it had become fully perpendicular to the cavern. The sudden stop jerked Seramin's shoulders painfully and fully half of the warriors that had clung to the ladder lost their grip and fell, slamming into the bridges below, crashing through the old wood and continuing their descent until their screams ceased. Seramin and the other warriors that had survived the ladder's fall risked a glance at the long distance beneath their feet, then began a frantic climb to the top of the ladder. The first one to reach a secure foothold would hold a staggering advantage over the other.

Higher up in the cavern Aagon made a stand in the middle of a bridge, battering warriors over the sides with his hammer. His movements were sluggish, and several attacks managed to make their way past his defenses. Cuts blossomed on the priest's arms. Gritting his teeth he slammed the warrior that managed to make a deep gash across his bicep over the railing.

Greot continued to climb, pushing away warriors with the tip of his axe. Holding on to a chain with one hand he slashed out with the other. Stuck in a difficult position the orc's attacks were poorly aimed and many bounced harmlessly off of his attacker's armor. He shouted for Shoshe and Snag Tooth to hurry. He could not hold them back much longer. The rat shoved and strained to move the much heavier girl faster. Unable to grab a secure foot hold the girl was moving much slower than he liked. "Move faster!" he shouted.

"I'm going as fast as I can!"

"Well, the black warriors aren't waiting for you!"

Back at the bottom Seramin and a single Northerner managed to climb to the top of the ladder. Lashing out with the silver sword Seramin aimed at the warrior's head, but missed by inches as the man ducked beneath the attack. The captain felt his feet slip on the tiny space that he was allowed to stand on. The ladder swayed back and forth as the two men battled against each other, each one's attacks awkward and uncoordinated due to their strange position. All the while Seramin tried to shut out the screams of the men that Aagon had dumped over the side of the bridge. Some of the human projectiles came so close that their clothes brushed Seramin's arms.

Taking note of this he waited until the next scream came and Seramin attacked from the barbarian's left, which forced the man to move in the opposite direction. A falling body clipped his hand, knocking the warrior off balance just enough so that Seramin could plant a boot into his stomach and push him over the side. Now unopposed, the captain moved about, knocking more of the warriors off of the ladder as they attempted to climb. Hacking at fingers and hands the sword left the frozen stumps still clinging to the wood.

A loud snap told Greot that something was wrong before he felt it. Suddenly the chain that he was holding on to became slack as the rusted pin finally surrendered to his weight. Unable to correct his position the orc tipped over the side, still clutching the chain in his right hand. As he fell more and more pins ripped out of the stone, causing Greot to fall even farther. After descending some forty feet the orc gave a violent jerk as one of the last pins in the chain held secure. He somehow managed to hold on to the chain throughout all of this, but, as the orc swung back at the cavern wall he saw a wall of steel instead of stone.

Kicking both feet into the nearest warrior Greot propelled himself back, and out of the range of the weapons. Several of the warriors from above rappelled downwards with their own chains, trying to attack Greot from all sides. They began a dangerous game of tag by jumping away from the wall, spinning and kicking as they went. The orc managed to knock two of the warriors away, but more kept coming. Several of the attackers tried to cut through Greot's chain with limited success, but the overwhelming power of the orc's axe proved to be more than sufficient in accomplishing this task. Sparks flew and a loud clang erupted as the blade of the green-skin's weapon snapped chain after chain in two.

Reaching a large metal cart identical to the ones found in the tunnel far below her, Shoshe grabbed its edge as the object swung dangerously from the chain that held it. "Hurry!" Snag Tooth pleaded. The Northerners were drawing near, and the Rotter knew that he couldn't hold them back.

"Just a minute," Shoshe snapped back, "as you can probably tell I don't do this much." Anger fueled her muscles to pull her up so that her head peeked over the edge of the cart, which was filled to the brim with gold and jewels. The girl's eyes sparkled with the sight of the riches, and her mind began to think about how she could grab a few coins for herself, but then she snapped back to reality with a squeal of pain from Snag Tooth. One of the warriors had managed to throw a dagger at him, nicking the rat in the thigh.

Looking from the cart to the rat Shoshe began to formulate a plan. "I have an idea."

"Don't wait too long!"

Pulling herself into the cart Shoshe clasped the pin that was wedged tightly into the chains that secured the cart, holding them in place. Bracing her feet she gave a mighty pull. The pin didn't budge. Sweating and straining at the pin Shoshe pulled with all of her might. It slid a little, but then stopped.

"Curses! Why won't you move?" she screamed and ranted as the stubborn pin refused to wield. "I want to live, gods damn it!" With a last pull Shoshe ripped the pin out.

As if in slow motion the girl felt the cart fall away from her. The extra energy from pulling the pin out sent her flying into the wall, where her head smacked into the stone. Stars burst as she bounced off and began to fall. Shouting a warning Snag Tooth snatched at Shoshe as she passed by, but his reach was too short. As she fell Shoshe's senses came back to her. Lying directly in her path was a bridge, its boards looking hard and solid. Her screams were cut short as Shoshe slammed into the wooden planks.

A shower of shining gold and glittering gems rained down the cavern, followed by a steel cart as it bounced and rolled from wall to wall, taking out bridges and scaffolding as it went. Men shrieked as they were pelted with the nuggets of gold and diamonds of various sizes. Many lost their balance and fell from their perches. The bouncing cart finished off the rest, destroying everything in its path.

The cart grew bigger and bigger in Seramin's vision as he looked up. The ladder was going to be crushed! Without a second thought he launched himself into the air, aiming for a small wedge that protruded from the rock wall. As he lost his momentum he felt himself falling downwards, slowing his advance towards the wedge. His fingertips brushed the rock, then managed to grab a hold just as the cart and its deadly shrapnel rushed past.

Finally, when the crashing of the cart had disappeared, all that remained was the curses of those Northerners that had been lucky enough to be standing near the entrance and had managed to dive back in at the first sight of danger.

The remainder of the climb proved to be tiresome, and quite dangerous as Aagon, Greot, and Seramin struggled to shimmy their way back to where Shoshe and Snag Tooth stood. A bloody gash had appeared on the girl's brow, but other than that she was no worse for wear. Aagon's body quivered with fatigue, and Greot's body was covered from head to foot with bloody bruises from bouncing against the rock wall as he had clung desperately to the chain.

They sat on the bridge, trying to regain their strength. Snag Tooth reassured them that it would take the Northerners many hours to reach them, assuming that they had incredible luck in finding the correct tunnels. After an hour Greot stood up without a word, took hold of Aagon's hammer, and moved to the steel door that connected to the tunnel. The priest did not object.

Pounding the door into scrap metal the orc motioned for Snag Tooth to lead the way. In absolute silence the group limped ahead, searching for a way out. Seramin did not know how long they walked, all he knew was that the tunnels they took sloped upwards, and that was all he cared about. Eventually they felt a cold breeze against their skin, and then, finally, after more than two days in the Ice Maiden (eight years for Snag Tooth), they emerged into the daylight: bloody, torn, and tired, but alive.

Chapter 21
End of the Beginning

With Yugarts patrolling the mountain it took a full day to escape. But, they were finally rewarded when the mountain began to grow smaller, and the tromping of Yugart feet could no longer be heard. They escaped from the Ice Maiden at dawn and they all screeched in pain from the burning sun as it rose into the sky; the rat the loudest. He had never seen the sun before and began thinking that it wasn't so great after all. Though after a while his eyes readjusted and he began asking all sorts of questions, such as what were those strange towering shapes (they turned out to be trees), and what was the white powder on the ground?

They put as much distance as they could between themselves and the Ice Maiden before dark. The silver sword kept Seramin from feeling the effects of the cold, but the others were beginning to shiver and they were forced to stop for the night in order to build a fire.

None could sleep. Perhaps they would never be able to sleep after what they had seen, and learned, inside of that mountain. They had all witnessed enough bloodshed and death to last a lifetime. Greot and Snag Tooth—ones who had grown up alongside warfare—were quiet as well. Seramin sat by the fire, twisting the Sword of Ice over in his hands, watching the fire as it reflected in the silver metal. There was an inscription in the metal. It was written in some sort of ancient text that he could not decipher.

Aagon took one look at it and whispered in a faint voice, "*Ikora' Majora*...The Elvish word for ice. It must be a Kirah!"

"Just like the sword Hydrib had."

"This sword was hidden by the gods themselves. It must be truly powerful."

"That must be why Hydrib attacked us. Having two of these swords would have doubled his power."

"Yes, but how did he get the other Kirah?" Aagon questioned.

"It's a mystery."

"Everything about that man was a mystery."

"Yes," Seramin agreed. His hand shot to his collar as he said it.

"What are you thinking about?" Shoshe asked, walking over to the captain and huddling up against him after Aagon had pulled away to discuss something with Greot, watching the fire as it ate the logs that Snag Tooth was throwing into the pit with great care. He let out a sigh. How was he supposed to explain his problems to an eighteen-year-old girl?

"We went through so much and all we found was this sword. We don't even know where this thing came from, or what its true powers are. It could be evil. All we know about it is that it was hidden by the sun gods and they didn't want anyone finding it. It turns Northerners into pretty good popsicles," he added as an afterthought.

"Maybe we shouldn't have found it," Shoshe suggested. "Some things are better hidden."

"Don't sound too disheartened," Aagon said. "Maybe there is more to the sword than we can see. Perhaps it will serve good instead of evil, as Hydrib's sword did."

"What do you mean?"

"Well, in the time that the gods walked amongst the mortals they created various magical items so that the humans could experience fleeting moments of god-likeness. It amused the gods so much to see their creations so powerful they began to make stronger and stronger items until they became so powerful that they feared that the humans that wielded these items would become gods themselves, and then the items were scattered across the globe and hidden. Some of them were buried deep into the depths of fortresses. That doesn't mean that it's a source of evil, but rather of great power."

"Could's the sword help you's to beat's the Northerners?"

"Yes," chimed in Snag Tooth, "maybe the sword will make you godlike."

"It doesn't matter," Seramin kicked at the snow in disgust, "the barbarians have pushed through the fortresses and have probably managed to flank the Southern army. I should have known it a long time ago. We've lost this war. What good would the sword be now?"

Shoshe's face broke out into an expression of shock. "How can you say that? You have committed your life to your country, to your family. You cannot just give up on them now. They need you... we need you!" She pointed at the other members of the group that nodded in turn.

"But... what can I do? What can one man do?"

"Look at what you've already done. You allied an orc, a rat, a priest, me, a blind girl, and... well, whatever Hydrib was. Who would think that any of us could amount to anything? Now look at what we've done. We've made it this far, now we must complete the rest of the journey."

"What if... What if I'm not strong enough?"

Seramin couldn't help but think of Hydrib. Dead. The great weapon that Terin had entrusted to him was now gone.

"Trust me, Seramin. You are strong enough."

A twig snapped in the darkness. Leaping to his feat Seramin gripped his sword, searching the forest for any signs of life. The air was now quiet again, but there was something out there.

"The Yugarts has followed's us's?" Greot asked nervously.

"They must have," Aaron muttered. "Do those things ever quit?"

Snag Tooth stuck his rat nose into the air and sniffed, searching for a scent. "I smell death," he said softly.

Now footsteps could be heard, slow and deliberate plodding as something drew closer. The survivors of the Ice Maiden backed away as the volume of the footsteps increased.

A pair of big black boots appeared, followed by pants that dripped heavily with blood. The man's chest was covered in blood and gore, and it shook with every breath. One hand held a massive black sword that was much too large for an average man to carry. Hydrib's face was covered in splattered blood, and an evil grin etched onto his face as a deep hunger burned in his black eyes. In an outstretched hand he held the severed head of a Yugart with curved horns covered in jingling ornaments.

Printed in the United States
62862LVS00003B/142-198